Il Alka E'Talania
(The Path of the Talonwood)

The Path of the Talonwood

Mythologia

Book 2

Jared N. Michaud

The Path of the Talonwood
Mythologia — Book 2

ISBN: 978-1-965598-09-2 ebook
ISBN: 978-1-965598-08-5 paperback
ISBN: 978-1-965598-10-8 audiobook

Cover Art
Dave Evans
https://ccworkfloor.artstation.com/

Interior Design
Jared N. Michaud
https://www.jarednmichaud.com

Other Works
by Jared N. Michaud

Energematrice6
Brightstar

From the Void

The Vale of Mysteries

Mythologia
Winternight

The Path of the Talonwood

Free Ebooks!
(And Value4Value)

The entire Energematrice6 library is available for free in ebook form at https://www.e6universe.com.

I offer this to you primarily because as a young person I wasn't able to afford to buy books, and was limited to what I could find at the library or, as I grew into my teens, online.

Please take advantage of it! Read everything!

If you enjoy my writing, I would appreciate it if you can return some value to me by buying something (like a physical book) to say "thank you" when you're able.

I hope you enjoy the world of Mythologia!

For Christ, who will always be my hero.

Acknowledgments

This is not a new story. As with Winternight, the first book in the Mythologia series, Path of the Talonwood was originally written in 2008, and my memory from that era is less than perfect. For that reason, I will inevitably forget to thank some of those to whom I'm genuinely indebted.

I do appreciate every single contribution and I am grateful to all of you, both named and unnamed, who contributed to this work.

Thank you all.

To Mary—You gave me time, even at the beginning, to write this. I still remember. You've supported me more than I could ever have asked. Thank you.

To my beta-reader-in-chief, Nick—I always aspire to catch your attention and your passion. Even when I don't completely manage it, I always appreciate your time and willingness to help me. Thank you.

To my lore collector, Multaan—You were busy. Again. And you helped me anyway. Again. Bless you. Your attention to detail always manages to uncover something I don't expect. Thank you.

To Luke—You've managed to point out the practical things, as ever. I appreciate the venom and all the other erratta. Thank you.

To Natalie—I've come to rely on you for more and more as time goes on. I'm proud of you. Thank you.

To Dave—You outperform each time you help me. First Winternight, now Path of the Talonwood. You've done an excellent job. Thank you.

To all of the folks who contributed in some way to this story over fifteen years ago when I first wrote it, thank you as well. As ever, here's to many more years and many more stories.

Finally, to the Father of the heavenly lights, you've given me so much. My words are not enough to thank you.

A soul of stone and ice had she,
The watcher of the wood.
And from it came a dark resolve,
To triumph as she could.
Though tried and tempted by the world,
Pursued by pain and strife.
Her courage polished,
By the cinders of her former life.
No crowd arrayed against her,
Could ever force her heart to yield.
No enemy could overwhelm her,
Though alone upon the field.

Prologue

The old man sat cross-legged with his back against the huge, polished granite column, his pipe clamped in his jaws, hands hanging loose in his lap. It was hardly fair, he thought, watching the elf maid reflected on the sheet of crystal before him.

She had already borne much, though she sat upon her horse proudly, unbowed. The girl—she was still a girl in his eyes—showed no sign that she realized anyone might be watching, which was as it should be.

If she had known what lay before her, it could have broken her... It still might break her. The old man could not see the future, whatever his powers. He was no wizard, simply a servant of a far greater master.

He knew what lay before her only because he could see the pieces of the puzzle more clearly than she. If life were a great game (it wasn't, however much *some* might think so), the board was stacked against her... except that she rode in the King's service, just as the old man himself did. That could make all the difference—if she allowed it to.

There was a ripple beside him and the old man looked over to see another illusion emerging, this one projected into the very air.

It was a black-cloaked figure, tall and arrogant, his face hidden but for red eyes that shone from the depths of his cowl. The surrounding gloom emphasized the aura of menace that hung about him, though the old man gave no sign he even noticed it. After glancing around, the figure took a moment to study the girl in the crystal, then laughed —a low, grating sound. "You would *watch* her ride to her doom, old man? At the price of allowing me to reach you?"

The old man smiled wearily and seemed to consider whether it was even worth stirring himself to answer. Eventually, he snorted dismissively. "Time will tell, Lorindar."

The dark figure sneered. "Surely you can't believe there's hope for her? She's entering my realm now, old man."

"Oh..." The old man's eyebrows rose in surprise and he gestured with his pipe. "You mean like she did in the North? Except that was your master's domain, not yours. Are you so much greater than he?"

The other gave no reply, but the menace surrounding him seemed to thicken, echoing emotions that were otherwise invisible.

After allowing the silence to hover long enough to make it clear he had no particular regard for anything the other might think, the old man smiled. "Time will tell."

Lorindar's angry retort came back almost instantly. "Whatever happens, she cannot escape. You know the depth of my... preparations. It must be torture for you, seeing her thrust into the heart of the furnace."

"You mean the same sort of furnace that an old man with a pipe saved her from once before?" The old man's expression was still deadpan, and nothing more than a slight curiosity colored his tone.

Lorindar grunted. His aura roiled in what must have been frustration, but his determination was unbowed. He changed tack. "You lost her father."

A flash of sadness crossed the old man's face, but he only cocked his head quizzically. "I feel sorrow for the lost, as do all the King's servants. That is no secret."

Lorindar sneered. "Your pity is weakness, old fool. She's going to die. Unless you risk yourself to save her again... and she's in my territory now, not the wretched Changers'."

The old man asked, with real curiosity this time, "Are you *trying* to get thrown out—again?"

This time, it was Lorindar who didn't reply for a long time. When he finally did, his response was subdued. "Would you lose your ability to watch her so easily?"

When the old man finally looked at him directly, blue fire crackled in his eyes. Neither spoke, but Lorindar soon vanished, leaving the old man to ponder the elf maid alone once more.

1.

Talina rode her mare stiffly, irritation spoiling her usually impeccable horsemanship as her mind was busy far away. She was not normally the type to brood, but her current mood was as close to it as she had ever been. The Deegani and their petty politics might just turn a routine succession into the end of the world. Talina let out a half-bitter, half-ironic snort and shifted in her saddle. Quite literally the *end of the world.*

She'd known Deegani were stubborn and self-centered, but the situation in Degan was so ridiculous it might have been amusing in other circumstances. As it was, the whole mess preyed upon her mind. Bretran's half-brother, Aratan, would have to wake up with a daemon standing over his bed before he took any notice of the parts of the world that did not orbit him.

Talina never thought it would be easy when they returned from the Madra'risa with news of the Nameless One's awakening. Telling the world what happened there on Winternight would be like telling a room full of trolls to do magic. Though they had learned the Nameless One was still alive and had seen his daemons face to face, it would take miracles to convince their respective peoples.

They only escaped from the great cavern above the Nameless One's prison with the help of Malakai, a messenger from... Talina shook her head. Could it really be the King of Yore? And, she thought, ruefully, he had made them promise to always call the creature Sheklah, rather than 'Nameless,' the appellation it had chosen for itself.

She had sworn allegiance to the King, as her people traditionally did when they came of age. Her people were the exception, however. By most races' reckoning, the King was dead, gone from Eschaton forever, or some sort of distant, uncaring deity, and certainly not a living man as Malakai said... And for all she knew, Malakai was dead— though she suspected he was too cunning to die so easily. More likely, he was either caught by the Nameless One— Shelkah's—minions or gone to a place only he knew.

The battle he fought under the Madra'risa, the black northern mountains, was beyond her comprehension. Talina was no sage; her ability with magic came in fits and starts. Her people's own greatest wise ones and sages could do nothing to help. In fact, they had never seen anyone with power as strange or temperamental as hers.

Despite all that, she could always tell when someone was using magic—and she could sense, more or less, how much they used. Talina had seen powerful sages at work more than once, but the energies she felt washing over her that night under the Madra'risa were incredible. Even now she could scarcely believe what had happened there. After they escaped from the hellish, black cavern, they rode back to Bretran's home, following a final encounter with some of Sheklah's minions.

That, of course, was when she met Aratan, Bretran's half-brother and the favorite to succeed his father to the throne. He had been oh-so-polite, even when they announced their finds in the North, then ignored them as much as possible. "Plenty of room for all in The North," he'd said lightly, pretending to jest while mocking laughter danced in his eyes. Talina could have spat—in his face. Nothing was more disgusting than a patronizing Deegani with a swollen head!

As Talina's mind ran back through the same loop she had been worrying at for the past week, a part of her still watched the world around her. She was an Aylf, a creature of the forest—born in the very Talonwood through which she traveled—and she spent the first turnings of her life learning its ways. The forest was her home, and she knew it well.

Even so, she never consciously realized what alerted her. It could have been a tiny sound, perhaps a movement, or even mere instinct. One moment she was sitting upright in her saddle, replaying the same stale thoughts, and the next, totally without conscious thought, she flung herself to one side and hit the ground, rolling into the brush.

The arrow meant for her thudded into her saddle, but she didn't have time to think of anything except her attacker. Where was he? Her gaze raked the forest... there! The black-clad figure knelt on the branch of a tree and pulled another arrow to his cheek, then loosed, already dropping forward off the branch to fall through the air toward her. Talina rolled to her feet and felt the wind of his arrow tickle her ear.

Another arrow buried itself in a tree a hand's breadth from her head as she dodged through the brush, and she stole a glance behind. Her pursuer was as quick and silent as she. She could see him, ducking around bushes in full pursuit. Turning to fight never crossed her mind. She had little training with a sword or knife, and didn't even carry a blade except her hunting knife. She was capable enough with a bow, but hers was on her horse.

Besides, suspicions already filled her mind about what her pursuer might be and she had no desire to find out. At best he was an assassin, and much as it horrified her, she could tell from the way he moved that he was probably another elf. Talina stole another glance behind her. She was gaining ground, but she needed to lose him. Spotting thick brush ahead and to the left, she swerved suddenly, putting a giant talonwood tree between herself and her pursuer. Then she threw herself head-first into a hole in the bushes. She landed and rolled to one side. There were no thorns or hidden brambles, she noted thankfully as she lay still, barely breathing. Her heartbeat thudded in her ears. She was starving for air, but dared not breathe any louder. She heard only a whisper, like the slightest wind stirring the leaves as he raced past. His movement through the brush disturbed nothing. Such skill could come only from long practice.

Her mind shied away from the other possibility. If it wasn't an elf... Visions of the dark creatures in those horrible northern caverns she so recently escaped flashed through her mind. That possibility didn't bear contemplation.

Quickly then, knowing there was little time, Talina stood and stepped to the bole of a tree. For a choking moment, she fought against panic and helplessness. Once her pursuer discovered he'd lost her, he would return to hunt her trail. All elves were trained in the ways of the forest to some degree. Even a child could follow its creatures by the trail sign they left behind. There were few trails that could be hidden entirely, and the thicker the forest, the more obvious they were.

Then she willed herself back to calm and purpose. She knew the best ways to fool a tracker, and there was only one rule: do the unexpected. There were, of course, small tricks she could use, ways to hide the marks she left behind on the ground, but she had a sinking feeling the physical trail she left would not be her undoing.

The lore of the Aylves, the tradition and collective wisdom of her people, taught another, more important trail: "Il alka e'cathri" —the path of the mind. To find the body, follow the mind. Know the objective, see the path. The question was where her pursuer would expect her to go.

Likely, he would first try to find her horse. By now Aolaira was long gone, headed for home without her. She had trained the mare well. If she was within a hundred leagues of home and fell from the saddle, Aolaira would go home without her—which reduced her possible destinations to one. It was a long three-day walk to Estaria, and she could not afford to lose time.

She had to go home first to get Aolaira, and home was the second place her pursuer would look for her. She could not do the unexpected. The best she could manage would be to take a roundabout route and still get there as quickly as possible. Simply striking out straight for home would likely be fatal. He would find and follow her trail far too easily. As she leaned against the bole of the old tree, considering, Talina took in the air and the spirit of the forest that was her people's ancient home. It had been too long since she visited.

These woods were the only place where the great talonwood trees grew. They were huge, many hundreds of links high with several distinct canopies of branches, growing much closer together and in more layers than should have been possible for such giants. Those canopies created several levels of interweaving branches that in ancient times had functioned as arboreal highways.

Of late, the elves had taken to walking the ground as the surrounding races did. Horses had provided a huge advance in how quickly the elves could travel, and they had tried for many turnings to train their mounts to walk among the great talonwoods. They failed every time—often spectacularly. So, the elves who used the talonwood highways were now nearly as scarce as those who still spoke more than snippets of their ancient native tongue. She could count the ones who did so frequently on just her fingers.

That arboreal legacy would be her escape.

A short while later, Talina was jogging easily along, hundreds of links above the forest floor, pacing herself carefully. It was several leagues yet before she would reach her destination, and leaving sign, even here, could easily be fatal. Nor were the talonwood roads themselves particularly safe—another reason they were perfect for her purposes.

A sudden thought gave Talina a little short-lived relief. When Aolaira arrived without her, her family would surely begin a search. Activity might frighten her pursuer off. If she could reach home, the assassin should think twice

before attacking. Her brothers were much more skilled
with bow and sword than she, and they would not take
kindly to someone trying to harm her... But she still had to
get there, and if she didn't hurry the assassin could precede
her.

2.

Hours later, long after night had fallen, Talina lay upon the branch of a great talonwood on the edge of the meadow surrounding her family's home. The meadow was one of those rare clearings that exist for no obvious reason in the middle of the forest. Instead of thinning out, the forest ended abruptly, giving way to a grassy hill upon which her distant ancestors had built their home. All around the clearing towered the Talonwood, the wall of greenery higher than the clearing was wide, and it was within this wall of living forest the killer would have to hide. If he was there, lying in wait, he would try to finish her as she crossed the clearing.

She saw no sign of her would-be killer during her trek through the branches of the Talonwood, however, and she had lain upon her perch for over an hour now, watching for anything out of place—any sign that enemies lurked nearby. There was none.

Slowly, still scanning her surroundings, Talina began to descend. When she reached the ground, she gave one long look around, then stepped from the forest and strode toward the house. Her instinct was to run for home and shelter, but something in her balked. Running from shadows showed weakness, and she was no mouse. If she was to die, let it be with her shoulders squared, walking toward her goal.

Besides, she thought, the skill her assassin had shown would make running pointless. On her way to the house, Talina neither hurried nor looked over her shoulder, but her back hunched involuntarily in anticipation of the arrow she half expected to come hurtling out of the darkness. No arrow came.

As she approached, her attention turned from the forest around her to the buildings, and she gasped aloud. In all the time she watched for her assassin, she had somehow neglected to study them closely, and now it was obvious to her that something was very wrong. The stables were too quiet, for one. The house was dark as well, not particularly odd for so late at night, but there was a stillness to it that was... out of place. Talina felt a finger of dread creeping up her back as she hurried to the door.

When she opened it, the smell stopped her as suddenly as if she had run into a stone wall. It was a smell of wrongness, of a dark evil that set her teeth on edge and made her stomach hollow. That scent had first come to her in the black northern mountains, in the same woods where she and her companions fled for their lives from the Sheklah's pursuing minions.

The smell was as foreign to nature as it was possible to be—the ancient, fetid stench of the perverted land that had once belonged to Sheklah. Only a few thousand turnings before, his warped magic had corrupted the people and creatures of the land he ruled into an army of hate-consumed demons. Some were taken against their will and twisted into malformed things—tortured and repulsive, desiring only their own deaths. Others... The worst of men had been his willing tools, and those he had remade—stretching and reshaping the bodies and souls of men and animals alike until they became his minions, remade to pollute and destroy the rest of creation.

Talina's vision was nearly as good in the darkness as in sunlight, so she could see everything as she opened the door and gazed into the entry hall. Nothing inside moved, and nothing seemed out of place—except a dark mound in the center of the floor. It looked like... oh dear Light!

Talina stepped forward and knelt, her heart skipping wildly. She reached out and slowly drew aside the cloak hiding the corpse's face.

It was her sister, Estella. Half of her face was gone, torn away, and what remained shone a sickly green. The wound was black and jagged, and the smell of poisonous death hung about her.

Talina leapt to her feet, her stomach trying to empty itself, mind rebounding in shock and pain. The move probably saved her life. As her head came up, she caught sight of two glowing red eyes in the shadows at the end of the hall.

The perverse, twisted smell increased threefold, and Talina reached blindly for the rack beside the door where her family kept the walking staves. The staves were nothing special to look at, but they had been formed from the seasoned wood of the oak trees that grew at the Talonwood's outskirts. Most were hundreds of turnings old, and they had been used as weapons on more than one occasion.

In front of her, a creature slowly emerged from the shadows. It was a Helthria, its cat-like frame covered completely in fine, black fur, its hindquarters tapering down to a tail tipped with a dagger-like sting. Talina's people did not purposefully teach their children about the Sheklah's creatures, but many of their legends and fables were based on the time of the Great War. If Talina's memory served as well as usual, the creature's tail and claws carried deadly venom.

The Helthria's red eyes were already focused on her, and it stalked forward another pace. It might have been breathtakingly beautiful, had it not been perverted into a foul mockery of nature's intent. Its streamlined body was designed for the pursuit and destruction of anything lesser —over land or through the trees. Legend said the Helthria's bloodline had been perverted from that of the Santhria, the mythical feline guardians of the Talonwood. It looked capable of moving faster than sight like a striking snake, and watching it left no doubt of the latent power in its wiry muscles.

Then its mouth opened and an unearthly screech filled the hall.

Baring its fangs, it leapt forward. Talina threw herself back out the door a split second before the beast's fangs closed where her shoulder had been.

Her staff came up and she struck at it. Her blow caught nothing but air, and she was barely able to bring her staff around to block the next lightning-swift strike from its paw. If the stories were true, she didn't dare take even a flesh wound. Those teeth and claws were as venomous as the tail that now came whipping down at her.

Talina could never remember how she survived the next minute or two. She only knew that she and the creature fought in circles in front of her family's home for seconds that seemed days. She was beginning to tire and became more and more desperate as the battle continued. She didn't dare turn to run. The thing would be more agile in the trees than on the ground. She had nowhere to retreat other than the house, and who knew what else might be inside?

It could only have been seconds before Talina found herself backed against a wall with the creature poised for a final leap. She slid sideways, trying to escape, and stumbled backward through the doorway. The creature changed direction to follow her, and she threw her staff at it like a javelin. The two met in mid-air, and the Helthria swatted the staff aside with the sweep of a paw, landing directly in front of her. Talina backed up frantically and tripped over her sister's sprawled body.

The creature hissed and spat as it stalked forward, stepping casually onto Estella, and Talina felt her eyes filling with tears of pain, sorrow... and rage as she held a torn and bleeding arm to her chest—an arm that she could not remember hurting. Already the flesh felt sick to her. If she could sense it, that almost certainly meant the monster's venom had some magical component rather than a simple physical toxin.

No, no, NO! This could NOT happen! She would NOT die on a cold floor to this gods-blighted creature! It killed her family, but it would NOT kill her. Not now. She could not leave her people, unsuspecting, directly in Sheklah's path. Talina's rage built until a red haze formed in front of her vision.

Curiously, in what must be her last moments, her mind seemed to retreat within her to all the memories she had shared with her family, and to growing up in the Talonwood. She remembered her first climb, the hours she had spent learning the ancient "il alka le'Enai," the ways of the forest, and Aylf lore. It had all come to this. Her life was done, her message still undelivered. It was NOT right!

The Helthria crouched, its tail poised to strike, and Talina cried out in despair and frustration, screaming words that she would not remember until much later, "Eanai! Eanai! Eanai al e'Ayaia! Tarios il Madradaria! Bicole Eanai o'Talania! Il'Feron, bicole e'Talan!" With her utterance, the creature hesitated, as if in surprise. With a screech it shrank back from her, eyes rolling in what was unmistakably fear. Then, turning, it leapt out the door, fleeing for the forest. Halfway across the clearing, something reached up from the earth, seized the creature mid-leap, and pulled it violently to the ground. Screaming in pain, the demon writhed and howled, dark vines like coarse ropes reaching from below to ensnare it and pull it down. Soon one limb was caught, then another. Before long, the Helthria was pinned completely. Then the writhing mass, now composed more of living forest than evil beast, began to contract. From her half-reclined sprawl, propped on one arm in the entry hall of her parents' house, Talina heard bones snap. One final anguished scream filled the air, tearing at the last of her sanity, and there was silence.

The forest, on the other hand, was not done. The mass of vines continued to writhe long after Talina had blacked out from pain, exhaustion, and relief.

3.

Three days later, Talina made painful progress along the road, leaning heavily upon her staff, her face turned toward the Aylvish city of Estaria. It was the only city the elves had ever constructed, built upon the hill whose name it bore and in the branches of the great trees above it.

She spent a full day removing her family from their ancestral home and burying them. After that, two more days of travel brought her almost within sight of Estaria. The entire time, almost minute-by-minute, she could feel the venom sapping her strength. At first, Talina had worried that she would encounter the assassin once more, but as the venom took its toll on her system, it was all she could do to press on, hoping her strength was sufficient to make it at all. Whatever her former assailant was doing, she had to focus just to keep moving forward.

Her whole family had been in the house except her brother Ciaran. Light only knew where he was. Her youngest brother was rarely at home, and dread filled her at the prospect of telling him what had happened. She couldn't even face her own grief now. The thought of watching him face his was unbearable.

At least Ciaran wouldn't have to see what the creature had done. The rest of her family had been mauled to death, and though the venom had begun eating their flesh—as it currently was her own arm—none of them had lived long enough to endure its long-term effects. Their bodies showed no sign of stiffening, which told her they had only been dead a few hours.

The worst... The worst had been Estella, for Talina saw something in her sister's one remaining eye that chilled her beyond reason. There was pleading, fear, and a bottomless grief there, as if she had looked for something beyond mortal life and found only pain and darkness.

All she could do was see that her family had a decent burial, despite the state the creature had left them in. Talina hadn't even gone near the stables. Her family alone was almost more than she could bear, and there was little doubt that her mare Aolaira lay somewhere around the barn. She had wept bitter tears as she buried them, but would have to take the time to truly mourn later. For now, she had to devote all her time and energy to saving her own life. None remained for grief.

Ironically, the place where the Helthria itself had died was now home to new life. A small sapling grew in the clearing before the family home. It was the rarest of rare occurrences—a new talonwood tree had been born. Talina's memories from that night were a mere patchwork from the time she opened the door to when the beast finally died. The battle, the thrown staff—everything was a blur. Talina couldn't even remember how she had survived. Obviously the forest itself awoke to the beast's evil in time to rescue her, though it had been too late to save her family.

Nor could she remember when the beast tore her arm. Beneath its dressing, the wound throbbed with every heartbeat. No amount of magical self-healing helped. Her magical abilities were as difficult and unreliable as ever, so that did not necessarily mean a great deal. She could only hope that her peoples' healers would be able to take care of it. Whatever the case, she could feel the toxins spreading through her tissue, and the pale, greenish cast of her arm frightened her. Her mind had begun to wander, as well. At times it was all she could do to maintain her focus and make steady progress toward her goal.

The venom was progressively sapping her strength. Talina was far too tired, and her brain struggled to make sense of the surrounding forest. She hoped once more that the healers in Estaria would be able to draw out the venom and mend her arm. Otherwise... Well, at least some form of rest waited at the end of this road.

And, thank the Light, the journey would not be long, she thought, cresting a rise to see the taller glade surrounding the elven city in the distance.

Upon entering Estaria, Talina gritted her teeth, heading straight for the Council Tree. The elves' great council was housed in the forest giant atop the hill, the only structure ever to have been constructed inside the bole of a living talonwood. Shaped from the heart of the massive tree by elf sages of times past, the tree was both the Aylvish seat of government and the repository for most of her race's history.

It was all she could do to keep herself focused on her goal as she made her way through the city. The Council Tree was so unique, it had become the Aylves' symbol among the other races of the world. It was also a fortress that had never fallen, even during the Great War when most of the forest outlying the Talonwood burned to the ground. Though most of the mighty talonwoods had been tormented with Sheklah's dark magic, no creature of the enemy had ever lived to breach the Council Tree. The magic that was used to shape it still lay dormant within, planted there to protect it from harm.

Deep in the pit of her stomach, she was afraid she had taken too long—that she wouldn't make it. A few other elves tried to greet her or offered aid, but their faces and voices blurred confusingly. She couldn't afford to be distracted, so she simply kept moving. It required tremendous determination just to stay awake. She felt weaker with every step now, and it was all she could do to stay upright.

At times, her mind wandered beyond her ability to control it, and she stumbled onward in a daze as events from the past replayed themselves or she hallucinated about the Enemy. It was outrageous that a demon like the Helthria could walk unhampered through the Talonwood while its master was still within the black mountains and not abroad in the world. It made the situation more dire than she had imagined, for the forest was both the elves' home and their most loyal defender. In a strange way, the forest itself was aware. It sensed the presence of intruders, especially those marked with Sheklah's dark touch. Such creatures were the enemies of every untainted living thing, and the Talonwood should have given warning, even if it did not turn on the creatures and destroy them outright.

If Sheklah's reach was so great now, what would it be when he did come forth from his mountains? Talina shivered, chilled by the thought... No, she thought sluggishly... The chill was fever... must be the venom. But she couldn't let that... or her wandering thoughts... keep her from reaching her goal. It would take a world united, fighting together, to stop Sheklah, when at the best of times uniting a single race or even a nation was a terrible struggle. And uniting a race was exactly what she had come here to do.

The first question, Talina thought, using her walking staff to hoist herself agonizingly up the last few steps up to the Council Tree, was whether anyone would even believe her. There was always grandfather of course. He had never doubted her word, but he was always so distant, wrapped up in his own affairs and those of the people as a whole. Her lips twisted ironically. Well, if this wasn't a concern for all her people, nothing ever would be.

Talina stopped before the huge double door set into the base of the Council Tree, gritting her teeth against her weakness, trying to focus despite the awful pain and sickness that threatened to take her from unfocused to incoherent. The door was sixty links high, but opened easily when she pulled on a handle at one side. Lurching through, Talina felt her wayward thoughts caught up in new wonder at the room before her. The entry hall was nearly as high as it was long, and the length of it filled most of the tree's girth. The walls were a glossy red-brown, rising to a vaulted ceiling fifteen stories up.

She remembered spending fascinated hours poring over the exquisite artwork and runes worked into them as a child... It was an ancient way of preserving knowledge, and from within the art, runes told the story of each illustration.

The most astounding thing about them was that the walls were not carved. They were grown into shape.

Her eyes traced the lines of the pillars spaced around the center of the room... They seemed to flow naturally up into the ceiling, their surfaces, like the walls, covered in scenes from Aelvish history.

Everything was made of wood, and it was beautiful... There were so many shapes and textures... Was it possible, Talina wondered, that her people had grafted the room together from other types of wood?

But no... her mind was wandering again... How long had she been standing there? She almost didn't care. It took so much effort to move... Better to stay for just a moment longer. She leaned heavily upon her staff, gazing at the floor before her... It was smooth and perfect despite the centuries of feet that had trod it. So smooth and dark... The end of the talonwood's grain was nearly as hard as stone.

She stood unmoving for several minutes, lost in her daydream... or was it a hallucination? Finally coming to herself once more, Talina felt fingers of panic clutching at her heart. She *had* to move. She forced herself forward, gritting her teeth as she advanced the staff a few links and was forced to bear her own weight again.

She had to tell someone—her grandfather, In'Kalith—of all that had happened! There were other elves around the room, some studying the runes and pictures, others speaking in quiet voices. As she half-stumbled toward the stairs, her eye caught one face in particular. A moment later, her brother Ciaran met her gaze across the entry hall, and he broke into a broad grin—that melted off of his face as he took in her state.

Forgetting his friends, Ciaran started toward her, calling at the top of his voice. "Talina! Talina? What's wrong?!" Talina sagged inwardly as the mental bonds holding her erect burst and she finally collapsed to the floor. It would have been hard enough to tell the Eldest, her grandfather. Ciaran was simply too much for her. His very presence brought back memories of the family she so recently buried, and the waves of grief she had pushed into the back of her mind refused to be held any longer. As her brother embraced her, Talina's body shook silently and tears streamed down her face. After a moment, Ciaran's face was all she registered, horror filling his eyes as he realized just how weak she was.

Finally, through her tears, Talina saw a tall figure descending the Council Tree's great spiral staircase toward them, then her grandfather was there, looking into her eyes, his expression grave. His solid, reassuring presence took immediate command and he reached out to take her up from Ciaran's arms. Through the darkness gathering before her vision, Talina heard him say, "... find healer Licia. This poison..." Talina's consciousness faded out. The last sound she heard was her grandfather's voice. "... will not live long."

4.

Of what happened after that, Talina remembered little. She knew only confused faces and the buzz of voices at a distance her mind could not seem to reach. It was as if she was being pulled down, deeper and deeper into herself. All she could feel was the venom eating at her, sapping her strength, wrapping itself around her like a malignant hand.

She must have slept after a time, for the next thing she saw was Estella's face, her single eye staring, gaze accusing. Voices buffeted Talina from every side, whispering in her ears of guilt and pain and hatred until she could hear nothing else.

Then the sounds stilled as if cut with a knife, leaving behind a deadly, painful silence. A figure appeared out of the murk in her mind.

It raised its head... and Lorindar stared at her like a midnight horror from the depths of the earth.

Lorindar's face had haunted her dreams as a child. To this day, she did not know how she knew it, but the face was his. She had described him to her grandfather once when she was young. It was the only time in her memory her grandfather had looked genuinely frightened, and he sent her to live with one of the sages for a time to ward her dreams.

Lorindar was exiled before her grandfather was raised to Eldest. Only a few knew why, even to this day, and she was not among them. She only knew he had been a great man in her great-grandfather's time, and then, at the height of his fame, he was exiled. She had thought him long dead. She knew that as a young man her father had certain dealings with him, and her father had been dead for many turnings.

His lips formed a word, and she felt it all through her as he said, "Mine... Mine! You are *mine!*" His fearful, terrible gaze seemed to bore into her soul and drew every dark desire and every fiber of hate and resentment in her to the surface, then fanned them into flame. One claw-like hand reached for her and she fled from him in terror, falling once more into darkness.

For a long time, Talina was barely aware, her thoughts pained and struggling. It was as if her mind tried to move through quicksand, and it pulled her downward, ever downward so that she could not breathe. She couldn't even think. Blind fear and pain held her fast.

The dream repeated.

Again, she saw her sister's face, then Lorindar and his beckoning hand and that single word, "Mine." Again, she fled into the darkness to escape.

She never knew how long she lay thus, asleep yet not, dreaming of the past, lost in a gloom of near unbeing. Through it all, she could feel the venom.

As it wrapped itself more and more tightly around her and she moved closer to death, a small, detached part of her could feel Lorindar's pleasure increasing. He was real, and he was alive. She could see through his eyes, deep into his desolate soul. It was he who, somehow, used the poison of the darkness in which she hid to tear her mind to pieces. It was he who tortured her over and over again with her sister's dead stare.

As the dream began once again and Estella's face appeared out of the confusion, Talina cried out for help. It was her mind screaming, in the horror of the dream world where time ran too slowly—too dreadfully—to bear.

Impossibly, someone heard her and another presence appeared beside her, comforting her, shielding her, separating her from the terror. There was a sense of age and wisdom. It took her a moment to recognize In'Kalith. Then Lorindar could no longer touch her, and her mind began to clear slowly of the fear and the darkness.

Lorindar knew it too, and this time, when his face formed, his expression had changed. Rage burned there now instead of hunger or pleasure. He reached out a hand to point at her and the presence beside her. "You! You shall not stop me, worm! She is mine!" The hand became a fist and lashed out. She could feel it battering the shield her grandfather held, again and again. It held easily, and Lorindar raised his voice in a language so ancient and evil its words twisted on his tongue, "Surrebai! Necalma a'Baross! Do calumier e Aynolae veritan! Baross de taroc A'nadua! MASTER!!!"

He fell silent and a shiver ran through him. Lorindar blinked and his head snapped back. A grimace of agony crossed his features, and his eyes opened once more, glowing red. The figure before her that had been Lorindar grew enormously. Instead of a thin, cloaked humanoid, a mass of deeper, blacker evil spread before her, edges blurring and shifting, as black as the surroundings but burning and distinct—and that gaze. Red eyes like solid hatred and pain transfixed her.

Then, it struck. The shield wavered, barely holding, and Talina felt her grandfather injecting his very essence into her defenses, straining to keep the monster without, both of them knowing instinctively that if In'Kalith failed, the consequences would be terrible.

In the moments before the next strike, Talina felt her grandfather's presence call out, crying for aid from forces she was unable to reach. Whatever he did, it came too late.

This time, it was not a fist that struck at the shield, but a blackness as sharp as a knife and as heavy as a mountain.

The shield shattered into a million echoing screams of pain.

In that instant, Talina felt a presence she had known as long as she lived disappear forever.

She cried out, fear beating at her, clutching her heart, an ancient fear with no end and no beginning—older than her people, older than Sheklah itself—fear more powerful than thought. Then, finally, another presence wrapped itself around her, vast and living. It was—it must have been —the Talonwood itself, enraged and grief-stricken, finally awakened by the death of In'Kalith.

The dream warped, stretched, and shattered, and Talina awoke. She couldn't see or even think, still gripped in her fear, and around her the room was black. A cry filled the night, the forest itself crying out for its lost. She too cried out in pain and loss, but in her cry, so deep and strong she was filled to bursting with it, was a terrible rage.

Elves did not anger easily, but Talina had been provoked beyond endurance, and a hand of ice closed around her heart. Her anger was not a quick, hot flame. It was ice and stone, as cold and hard as the fabled ice mountains at the top of the world, and just as enduring. Her body, on the other hand, was still weak. Utterly exhausted, she sank back into sleep.

5.

The room was dimly lit when Talina awoke, weak but immediately alert. Around her she could feel the Council Tree, and beside her... beside her sat Ciaran. Her grief came back anew, but it was overwhelmed by the cold rage that still gripped her heart. Neither was more than she could handle now, though. She was rested, and her arm had healed. She could tell without even moving. No pain or venom clogged her system. Ciaran's head had nodded forward against his chest, and he was obviously asleep. Talina moved a bit and his head came up. He blinked and stared at her.

"Talina! You're awake. It's been so long, and after what happened three nights ago they were afraid—well, we were all afraid your mind... but you're obviously awake, so you can't be..."

Talina laughed, half in amusement and half in irony. It startled her that she could still laugh, but it was the right thing to do, and her heart grew lighter within her. Talina reached down to uncover her arm, revealing a deep, scarred fissure where the damage had been before. She shook her head as she studied the now-healed wound, a wry twist to her lips. "Slow down, Cee. I'm not going anywhere."

"I suppose not..." His eyes widened. "But you don't know about In'Kalith either."

Talina touched his hand, and said, half in sadness, half in anger, "Yes, grandfather is dead. The council will need a new leader—very soon."

She looked at him for a long moment, then took a deep breath and began what she knew would be the hardest conversation she'd ever had, "There's more you need to know. It will take some explaining, but our family..." Talina trailed off, pain filling her to bursting. "They're dead, Ciaran. They were killed by a demon—a Helthria."

Ciaran read the truth in her eyes, and he turned white. "What?!?"

It took over an hour to explain. By the end, Talina's heart was a ball of solid ice within her. Recounting the experience for her brother was like reliving it, and her sorrow had congealed into iron against those who were trying so hard to destroy all she loved.

Ciaran stood at her side with his hand on her arm, and as she looked up into his face she saw his warring emotions. Despite the obvious sympathy in his grip, his face was white and she saw something hard and cold in his gaze that matched her own rage.

"And you're sure—you don't know who the assassin was?" Ciaran's tone mirrored his stare.

Talina shook her head, wearily. "No. He wore a mask, and I had no notion at the time of what he'd done. Even if I had..." Talina groped helplessly for words.

"Whoever killed our family, I swear, when I find him, I will claim Il'Andama!" Ciaran's voice was raw.

Talina sighed, dropping her head and closing her eyes. Il'Andama, the challenge of the wronged, had only been invoked a few times in her people's history. It was a rite of single combat, called upon as a last resort to see justice done when no other recourse was available. Actually finding the culprit might be impossible, but if he did, she had no doubt he would do precisely that. She would just have to make certain he chose the right target for his wrath.

When she looked up, Ciaran was turned half away from her, staring into nothing. Seeing the hard, cold blankness in his stare, she understood why the giants said an elf with a cold heart was the creature most to be feared in the world.

6.

Hours later, Talina stood silent before the leaderless council, seated in a semicircle. The position of honor in the center remained empty, as In'Kalith had left it.

The council was in a delicate position now, too weak to remain leaderless for long, considering the news she had for them. Aside from the simple fact that there were only twelve members and no way to break a tie vote, by elvish law they could not make binding decisions of any consequence without an Eldest. Everyday affairs were within their purview, but certainly not a decision to prepare for war against the darkness gathering in the north.

Talina had once considered taking over the eldership when her grandfather's time came. Some of her family's friends and allies had even encouraged her to do so during her youth. That ambition had been crushed when In'Kalith himself declared with an unfathomable gleam in his eye that she would be neither Elder nor Eldest of the Talonwood.

As she grew older, she realized he was right. She had neither the desire nor the temperament to become an

Elder. She had been a wanderer for most of her life. The Talonwood might be home, but she would never be entirely comfortable here. No, she had no interest at all in building consensus, forging alliances or resolving the disputes of the rest of the community. When she made decisions, she made them quickly and without the deliberation—what looked to her like quibbling—that her people's representatives were so often caught in. In short, she knew she was not the shepherd her clan, Anisa, needed.

Despite the council's weakened position, however, her people still had a right to know of the monumental events in which she had been embroiled in the north. The news of her return and her request to address the council had spread like fire in a tinderbox. The room at her back was full. In the front rank stood Ciaran and the two friends she had first seen him with in the Council Tree. Sestan was a member of the Garik clan, grandson of Elder I'Nakima, who would now temporarily preside over the council after In'Kalith's death. Calista, also of Garik, which was the most numerous, was not Sestan's sister, but, Talina was told, the two were so close they might as well be siblings.

The council room held no seats but those for the council itself, and the floor sloped steeply back for several links to leave a dais for any speakers and the council. This room too had been created with exquisite care, leaving the slope showing the end of the wood grain just as the rest of the room. It was for even wear and an attractive finish, but it gave the appearance that there was no slope at all. Unless one knew how the room was built, seeing someone apparently stand above floor level to address the council could cause some confusion... not to mention the tripping hazard, she thought, smiling slightly.

Elder I'Nakima, now the longest-serving of the council members, wore an expression that was positively grim, likely because of In'Kalith's passing. In her hand was the staff of Elders, which tradition said had been given to Warden Ay'Thera by the great Wizard himself. It was normally held in trust for the people by whoever headed the council.

The staff was grown from a living talonwood sapling, long frozen by unfathomable power in a form that could be held in the hand. Some said it was imbued with the very life force of the forest around them, which kept it alive despite being long cut loose from any root. Green shoots sprouted from the top, growing into a tight pattern that created a symbol of many intertwined circles. The rest of its length was the same texture as the horny bark of the talonwoods, miniaturized to create a gripping surface for the hand.

For most elves, the staff was nothing but a fancy stick—except that it couldn't be broken by any known force, magical or physical.

For the Eldest alone, it provided a link to the Talonwood and granted certain powers over the forest. It was said that through the staff's power, intruders into the Talonwood could be made to feel very unwelcome indeed.

I'Nakima raised the staff, calling out the traditional greeting. "Arios o'con i vilana is'ona le'Ayaia." *Draw near and take heed all ye of the true People.* The ritual words had been used to open the council for as long as anyone could remember, as had those she next spoke. "Fera son sidua ana ye'pala, ey na vila." *Be there any who would speak, let them be heard.*

I'Nakima sat and lowered the staff, leaning it against the chair to her left, which was normally occupied by the

Eldest. "Talina ne'al Kalin ni'al In'Kalith, you come before us at one of the gravest times in modern memory. The Eldest lies dead, slain by we know not what. Rumors of gathering darkness reach us even here. You came to us wounded and sick with poisons the healers have never encountered. What have you to say?"

Talina looked around the semicircle of Elders, catching each one's gaze, then began, "Ayanorionae le'Enai, when I left you I set out hardly knowing what I would find, or even what I was looking for. What I discovered leaves me with a dread so strong I can hardly express it, and even here events have already progressed further than I had feared..."

It took several hours to tell them what happened since Winternight, then several more to answer the innumerable questions that followed. Yet Talina didn't think a single elf left the chamber the entire time. Going back over it all was both a strain and a relief. Though she had rehearsed over and over in her mind, it was difficult to retell the story to those who had not experienced it, and she struggled to capture the urgency she knew was needed.

When there were no more questions, I'Nakima, who had been curiously silent during all the questioning, stood. "In view of these circumstances, I believe the position of Eldest must be filled as soon as possible. To that end, I urge Anisa to choose its new Elder with all haste. This council stands adjourned."

7.

After she spoke to the council, Talina walked outside for the first time in days. Strolling across the terrace around the Council Tree, she shook out her hair and felt the breeze. Even in Estaria City proper, nature was everywhere. Right now she wanted nothing more than to hike into the Talonwood outside the city and take in the peace of the timeless, ancient forest, but that was not to be. Clan Anisa was to have its meeting at the Aeth al'Miera, the only place more sacred to the elves than the Council Tree itself. It was in the Aeth, the histories said, that the first of the Aylves had assembled to pay their respects to the departed Sidhe. Since that time, all ceremonies of importance—especially the choosing of new Elders—were held there.

Talina was thinking about the situation with her family and clan so deeply that at first she didn't notice when another elf fell into step with her. When she did see him, her hand went to her mouth in embarrassment. His smile carried deep, lurking amusement. "I apologize, Neyona. I didn't mean to startle you." His mode of address surprised her, at first. It was a mark of respect, a term from the Old Tongue meaning something like 'my lady.'

Talina shot him a sideways glance and a wry smile. "I fear my awareness is not what it should be, Niyone. My teachers would be ashamed."

He made a throwing-away gesture, shaking his head. "You have a great deal on your mind. The fault is mine. I am Janrae of Orlon." He bent slightly at the waist, offering her a bow, and Talina nodded. She remembered him, both from the council meeting and many years before. He had been an associate of her father's, before...

A sigh escaped her at the memory and Janrae's smile slipped into ruefulness. "I'd no intention of adding to your burden, Neyona. Your pardon." He started to move away, bowing once more.

Talina shook her head. "No, Janrae. Your company is welcome. I've been alone with my thoughts too much of late."

The smile returned and he nodded, falling back into step beside her. "The news you brought us from the north is most disturbing, Neyona."

Talina nodded, but now it was her turn for a rueful smile. "It is, but I fear my thoughts this day were more for my own family and clan Anisa than Sheklah. It has been two thousand turnings since my family had no one to sit as Elder for Anisa..." or even, she didn't say, alive. Again, pain and anger pulled her lips into a tight line.

Janrae looked at her in astonishment. "You mean, you don't intend to stand for Elder?" He shook his head. "And I would think, after all you've endured, you would be more cautious than most, using the Byzimyanny's own name, Neyona."

Talina laughed, grimly. "We who belong to the King need not fear the Disturber's attention. So I was told by Malakai himself. As to the eldership, In'Kalith told me long ago that I would be neither Elder nor Eldest of the Talonwood, Niyone." She shook her head. "I'll not dishonor his memory."

Janrae nodded, raising an eyebrow in question, and asked, "What of your family, then?"

Talina shook her head. "My family is just me and Ciaran, now. We have no other." She paused, troubled. Normally, under such circumstances, their nearest kin would take them in, but her family had no other branches, and their nearest kin were very distant indeed. She looked over at Janrae, eyes hooded. "It may very well be that *you*, though you are of the Orlon clan, are our nearest kin, Niyone. We have no tribe either. Our family has not divided in two thousand turnings, and the rest of our Tribe was killed during the Separation." Elvish families were tight-knit, relying on each other for shelter and protection. They were the bedrock of society. Not having a family—or a tribe, a closely related group of families—put both her and her brother in a dangerous position.

Janrae hesitated, then nodded grimly in sympathy. "You would be welcome in my house, Talina. You may not remember me, from so long ago, but you played with my own children, before..." He gestured with one arm, as if sweeping something away.

"I would not leave Anisa without guidance if there is any choice." Talina stopped and laid a hand on Janrae's arm. He was tall and heavily muscled for an elf, and he towered over her. She smiled sadly up at him. "I thank you, Niyone. You are more than kind. Grandfather—In'Kalith, and In'Lokrim before him—were both Eldest who came from our family. Anisa has long relied on us, and I fear without the rest of my family, we may leave the clan to trouble... or even dissolution, if I accept your offer."

Janrae's breath hissed between his teeth as she walked on and he fell into step beside her once more. The dissolution of a clan was exceedingly rare in elvish history and hadn't happened since the Separation, when the elves had been scattered across the face of Eschaton. Many had been killed in the Great Pogrom, in which the were-men, still loyal to Sheklah, had captured and massacred entire tribes of elves. He shook his head. "Surely not. We were leaderless, the last time that happened. We were scattered, and with no council. Surely no one would wish Anisa dissolved."

Talina laughed, darkly, "I fear we Aylves are too bound by tradition and not enough by practicality, Janrae. My family has not had a tribe in almost a thousand turnings, yet we remain our own solitary branch of Anisa's tree. We have grown steadily fewer, yet we have been allowed to lead not only Anisa, but the entire council, for almost that whole time. We go on, even when we shouldn't."

Talina looked over at him. "I've told you why I cannot be Elder for Anisa, and Ciaran... much as I love him, he is... too young."

Janrae laughed in turn, and she was surprised to realize that his tone echoed a bit of her own grimness. "Young may not be the word for it, Neyona. It isn't my place to say, but in truth you are right. He is not suited for it. He is ambitious and has poor judgment."

She looked over at him in shock and he laughed again. "My forthrightness surprises you, Talina? I know we Aylves have a tendency to stand on ceremony, but as you pointed out to the council, we can ill-afford it now."

Something inside her eased, and she sent him a deeper, more genuine smile. "You're right, Janrae, but it takes a brave man to make real advances away from custom toward sensible action."

He smiled back with raised eyebrows, "And a brave lady to tell the council all you did and give us the impetus to take action at all." There was genuine respect in his tone, and his next words were solemn. "I had thought—hoped even—that you would assume leadership of both your clan and the council with In'Kalith's passing. I understand your reluctance, but surely..." He trailed off, giving her a lingering look.

Talina sighed. "There is more to this than just my wishes, or even In'Kalith's, Niyone. His words were spoken, not in admonishment, but in prophecy. I will *never* be either Elder or Eldest of the Talonwood."

Janrae's expression settled into deep disquiet, and they walked in silence for a long time before he said, "We have no wars of succession. We haven't even seen deep divisions among the People since the Regathering, but this... We elves are far too stubborn and arrogant, Talina. I fear where these currents may take us, especially if what you said about the Byzimyanny..." he paused, then corrected himself grimly, "... about Sheklah, is true."

"I know." Talina gazed up at him once more, her thoughts now turned inward. "My family is gone, Janrae, all except for Ciaran and me..." She sucked in a breath, then spoke what was in her heart. "Too much has happened. I've barely had time to breathe, much less find my center."

Tears glittered behind her eyes, and her voice was brittle. "I have no time, even to grieve. There *IS* no time."

Janrae stopped and laid a gentle hand on her shoulder, stopping her in turn, "When you've need of an ally, remember me, Talina. Regardless of what happened in times past, I was your father's friend. I am honored to be yours also." He squeezed her shoulder, then grinned. "But now, I should be going. I might very well *start* a war of succession if I accompany you to Anisa's gathering. I doubt they would accept your fanciful notion of me being your kin."

Talina laughed in turn, returning his grip with a squeeze of her own, and nodded.

When Janrae turned away, however, Talina felt once more the rage within her core. She had left the Council Tree seeking some vestige of calm from her own internal storms, and as heartwarming as Janrae's company had been, she still hadn't found her center.

A small part of her knew she could ill-afford her emotional upset, especially her rage; it would cloud her judgment. She desperately needed time to make peace with all that was happening, but the larger part of her had ceased to care. There was nothing she could change about her situation or what the rest of the clan did, and that merely fueled her frustration and rage.

When Talina entered the Aeth, she was still searching in vain for the peace of the forest.

8.

The Aeth al'Miera stood in the undisturbed Talonwood beyond Estaria. It was only a short walk from the Council Tree, but the elves avoided that part of the forest unless they had a specific reason to go there. Respect for the legends of their past had kept the Aeth and its surroundings pristine.

If the rest of the forest was ancient, the Aeth was old beyond memory. Its trees stood many hundreds, even thousands of links high, and in the center, far shorter than any of the trees but more massive, stood the grave of the ancestors. No one knew precisely what the grave was, other than a mammoth pile of stones. It was said the first of the elves lay buried there. The site was certainly a center of great power. Even Talina, with her small, undeveloped talents, could feel it around her, solid, strange and implacable. She'd heard that many sages could see magic all around the place, in the trees, the rocks, and even the air itself, but that even the great sages couldn't manipulate it. She had never seen magic, but she could feel the power, and in the Aeth it was everywhere. Unlike the magic of the Council Tree, though, this power was not friendly or protective. It simply rested there—a huge, uncompromising force, as irresistible as the tide.

Before the grave, Anisa had gathered. It wasn't everyone, of course; the heads of all the families had come to tend to clan business. She knew most of the hundreds of faces from her childhood, but some were new.

Each of those standing before her had at least twenty who looked to them as the head of the family. The average was probably closer to sixty or eighty. Her family had been small by elvish standards even before Sheklah slaughtered them.

Talina saw questions in the faces of that crowd. They could not know any more than she did what was going to happen, and, she admitted to herself, they had to be as worried as she—about the fate of the clan if nothing else. Somehow, though, the burden of the whole race seemed to fall on her shoulders alone. Perhaps it was that only she had seen Sheklah's prison and the weakness of its seal, but when she put the situation in perspective, even her own troubles and those of her clan shrank to nothing next to what faced the Aylvish race as a whole.

The clan was still milling about when she arrived, though it was holding roughly to the customary half-moon shape, edges against the grave with a shallow arc of clear space left for those who would speak. Voices were hushed, as the occasion also traditionally marked the passing of the previous Elder.

Besides, she thought, a feeling hung about, an almost tangible calm before the storm... or impending doom.

Talina stood at the edge of the crowd, simply waiting, allowing the breeze to flow over her and taking in the forest. This was right. Somehow, despite the almost electric feeling in the air, this was right. Except... Except... Then it was gone.

So it had always been with her magic. Any power she might have inherited from her father always impacted her so. She saw, in that moment, a seed of darkness among them, understood what it was and how it would manifest, then in the same instant completely lost that understanding. Her power, the Elders and sages said, was as hidden from them as it was from herself.

She watched as the gathering quieted, allowing her mind to clear. Eventually, N'Ahlren, head of the largest of Anisa's families, stepped forward to speak. Normally, the new head of household from the last Elder's family was the first to address the clan, but this was hardly a normal circumstance. Nor had she jumped forward to do so.

Unsurprisingly, N'Ahlren wished to take the position of Elder for Anisa. They could have worse, Talina supposed, though N'Ahlren had always seemed a bit thoughtless—for an elf.

N'Ahlren finished speaking, and Talina noted with some relief that the crowd seemed less than enthused by his message. A few were having their own conversations, none-too-quietly, and many of the rest were obviously bored. Another stepped forward to speak, and, with a start, Talina saw that it was her brother Ciaran.

He stood before the assembly, head bowed, then slowly raised his face to the crowd. Come to think of it, she and Ciaran had not actually agreed who would speak for them. She had simply assumed she would, being the elder sister. Apparently, he hadn't agreed, or even thought it prudent to talk to her at all... and that was worrisome.

"I come before you with little enough to show," he said, "other than a good heart and, of course, the tradition of my fathers. As you well know, it has been a thousand turnings since another family claimed the seat of Eldest, and longer still—from before the Separation—since one not of my family sat for Anisa.

"Many of you are willing to take either of those positions if you must, but please, consider." His gaze raked the gathering, intense and demanding. "In these times, who better to speak for us than we who have always done so? Who among you has been trained from birth in the ways of leadership?"

He paused to look around at the gathered clan. "Who can truly claim more right to the position than we? I leave it to you, but I ask, do not let my youth trouble you. Grandfather and I became... close... before the end of his life. I may still have learning to do, but I believe now more than ever Anisa must hold to our time-tested ways and traditions."

Talina's brows rose in astonishment. Unless things had changed dramatically—more than she'd thought possible— her brother never got along with In'Kalith. They were too alike in some ways, too different in others, and In'Kalith never seemed to like Ciaran—which was unusual for her grandfather. She glanced over the crowd. Most of those around her stood in thoughtful silence. A few were nodding, but none seemed troubled. The situation had, indeed, changed since Talina left if Anisa was ready to accept one as young as Ciaran for their Elder. Talina saw Sestan and Calista, Ciaran's friends from Garik, standing near the edge of the crowd. That was more than a breach of etiquette, Talina thought with bemusement. They were hardly forbidden by law from coming to Anisa's gatherings, but it just wasn't done... certainly not without overriding reason.

The understanding she'd momentarily experienced, of the kernel of darkness within her people, coalesced once more for Talina, and at first she gasped in disbelief. Ciaran? Surely not!

But it fit too well. He had never talked this over with her, and... and something about his friends being here, at Anisa's clan meeting, left her with a sinking feeling—and a duty. Ciaran was her responsibility. She couldn't allow this.

Talina stepped forward, pushing through the silent crowd. As she cleared the front ranks, she said, "My brother, why would you take this action without speaking to me first?" She paused as she entered the clear area before the others, searching his face. "And your friends? What business has Garik at Anisa's council? It is not right."

She stepped forward and opened her mouth to continue, but Ciaran cut her off, "Go lie down, sister, this does not concern you. You may mean well, but now is hardly the time for such nonsense."

"What?!" Shock seized her once more and she gaped. "What are you talking about?"

His voice took on a harshness she had never heard from him before, and his next words were spoken to the crowd, though he addressed himself to her. "We all know what you said to the council yesterday, and in your condition?" He shook his head, almost pained. "Please, don't make this harder than it must be."

Talina's mind reeled. What was wrong with him? She felt a tug on her sleeve and glanced back to see Ciaran's friend Calista beckoning her away, a pained look on her face. Another look at the crowd around her left her with the grim realization of how little she knew her people. Hostile glares assailed her from every side, demonstrating how effective Ciaran's words had been. Were the elves—and her own clan Anisa—so easily fooled? Was her brother so power-hungry? Or did he believe she was... well... crazy?

Lost in shock and uncertainty, Talina allowed Calista to lead her away, still unable to cope with this new revelation.

She had been so focused on the events of Winternight, so caught up in the need to warn her people of the impending darkness. Then, when she was nearly killed by the Helthria, well... It had never occurred to her that her people's reception might be outright hostile, especially after Janrae's warmth.

But of course it would be! What had been a sinking feeling in her gut dropped away, leaving her with a momentary sense of being in free-fall. She had seen the reactions among the Deegani, Bretran's people—and people were people. She had miscalculated more horribly than she would ever have thought possible. Bitter hindsight told her that Janrae had sought her out because he understood that.

Outside the Aeth, beyond the first ring of talonwood trees, Talina stopped, bringing Calista half way around to face her. "Do you believe it?" Talina asked her, quietly.

"You've been gone... for a long time." Calista wouldn't meet her eye. "So much could have happened... and a story like that." She shook her head slightly, then met Talina's gaze, her face impassive. "I'm sorry, Neyona. No. Ciaran didn't think it possible that you would come back just to... to try to steal the position from him, but after what happened to your grandfather, well, he couldn't let you."

Talina sucked in her breath between her teeth, "You're not suggesting...?!"

"I only know what people are saying." Calista's lips thinned. "You must admit, the timing was... convenient, and Ciaran said you *knew* In'Kalith was dead before he ever told you."

"Yes, but—"

"And your family... well... Ciaran rode back to your family home himself. He told us what was there. That's enough to drive anyone a little mad. Besides, if the Byzimyanny were really coming back there would be signs. Even the least truthful of the old stories tell of signs..." Calista shrugged, but her lip curled scornfully. "There just isn't any evidence."

Talina gazed into the other woman's face, and when she spoke, her voice was hard. "I know what I saw. It was no illusion, and if any of you were truly looking you would see it as well. Have there been no signs, then? What of the night In'Kalith died? Did you dream?"

Calista flinched, then shook her head, "Dreams... aren't real."

"And dreams are not signs? Tell me, if you know so much of signs, what were the first signs the last time Sheklah turned its attention upon the elves?" An edge of anger had crept into Talina's tone. "No? Well, I'll tell you what they were. Our people were troubled by voices in their dreams telling them not to trust their neighbors... or their husbands... or their brothers. Friends betrayed friends.

"After that, the treachery and the murders began. Tell me, Calista, which of those signs are missing?"

Without waiting for an answer, Talina turned and strode toward the Council Tree, rigid with fury. The daylight, while unchanged, suddenly seemed much darker, and she could almost see Lorindar's laughing face before her.

9.

That night, Talina sat in her guestroom in the Council Tree. She didn't ask not to be disturbed, but she felt sure none of the other elves would do so. Only a few had spoken to her at all for the rest of the day, and she felt far more alone than she ever had during her long absence from the Talonwood. At least then she'd had Aolaira.

That thought brought too much pain... and led to too many memories. She stifled it instantly... almost instantly, but then Estella's face appeared, ruined and accusing, and without warning the sobs she'd been holding back for days burst from her.

How long she cried, Talina didn't know, but it seemed to last forever. All the grief she'd held in and the pain she'd hidden away came bursting out like a river flooding through a broken dam. Despair seized her heart with fingers of steel.

An undefinable time later, as if in a place and time a long way off, she felt a gentle hand on her shoulder. A moment before, she'd have thought herself incapable of any movement at all, but then, without conscious decision, she was on her feet facing the stranger. Even through vision blurred with tears, she could see that he was an old man. In'Kalith had been old, even by the standards of the elves, but the man she saw standing before her was—had to be—older still. While he still looked able and strong, his hair was pure white and... Talina couldn't make sense of the feeling, even to herself, but he *felt* ancient, almost in the same way as the great talonwood in which they stood.

His eyebrows rose at her quick movement, and he quirked his mouth in a half-smile. "Are you well, then?"

"I... I... Who are you?" Talina's grief had subsided with her alarm. The demands of the moment seemed to do that at times. Even then, taking in her unannounced guest, she fought the pain down as it continued to well up again inside her.

"I, Neyona? I am Cain." Seeming to sense her internal agony, he again laid a hand on her shoulder. Talina felt a shock go through her, and immediately her sorrow began to ease. It was still there, but lessened. It was as if, once spent, it had found its true place inside her. She still felt the same pain, sorrow, hatred and anger, but the raw edge where it felt as if someone had torn a piece from her soul was healed.

She looked at him, surprised, "What did you do?"

His half-smile turned up at one corner until he looked half-sad and half-amused. "I showed your heart what your mind could not yet see." He shook his head slightly, and the smile turned rueful. His voice took on a more serious edge, however, one that forbade further inquiry, when he said, "I'd ask you not to pursue that any further. Some things are not mine to tell, as yet."

Then he seemed to shrug off his misgivings and his tone was light again. "It might be better, I think, to ask not who I am, but what. That question is difficult, but not too difficult. The easiest answer would be to say I am 'Il Ania le'Aynoria'—Keeper of the Histories."

He smiled, "But for you, I think the easiest may not be the wisest. I am, as you can see, quite old." He nodded, as if hindsight had confirmed something for him. "I spoke with your grandfather often, you know. We shared a great deal, him and I." A shadow came over his face, "Perhaps too much. I long ago learned to be careful what I share with whom... I should have learned, that is." His smile reappeared as if it had never left his face. "Would you like to see what I'm working on today? I thought you might wish to break up the monotony of the evening, as I doubt you have had much to do since that farce before the Aeth al'Miera le'Bicola."

Talina frowned. "le'Bicola? Of the guards?" She paused, then shrugged. "And yes, I would love to occupy my mind with something... else."

"Guardians. The Glade of Ancient Guardians would be a close translation I suppose, but this modern tongue misses so much of the real meaning behind such names. A complete translation might be, 'Glade of the Ancient Guardians who are not yet fully revealed, but stand always in defense of the true People.'"

He paused, looking thoughtful. "When you've lived as long and studied as... obsessively as I have, you'll find that language carries meaning on its own." He paused and gestured for her to follow him out the door. "That is, after all, its purpose. Words have life. Did you ever hear a word and you knew exactly what it meant without ever having to ask? Some languages are stronger than others, but they all speak on their own." He chuckled and shook his head ruefully. "I can see without even looking that you must doubt me, but consider: When you speak to children do they truly have to find references for all the words they encounter? It hardly seems possible that they would. The subtle magic behind the world we live in is much harder to understand than most would believe.

"The language we use now is near to dead." Cain made a face, as if the words coming out of his mouth disgusted him.

Talina cocked her head, "Dead? Why is it dead?"

Cain shrugged. "I am not sure. Too new? Untried? Perhaps it simply isn't close enough to what language once was? The Old Tongue, on the other hand..." He shook his head, paused, and sighed. "Most don't even realize what we've lost." He looked back at her with an unspoken question and they lapsed into silence for a time.

Talina frowned. "You said your name was Cain? That name is rare among us. I might expect it of the Deegani, but..." She shook her head. "I have heard of none among our people who bear that name since Ay'Thera's time. Even during the Separation, what parent would dare? How did you come by it?"

He chuckled—a rich, melodious sound. "You seem to have a way of coming right to the heart of a matter, Neyona."

He let a silence linger, then sighed. "Yes, Cain was the name of Ay'Thera's... murderer, it is true. My parents were not friends of Aylvenkind. They wished me to carry the legacy of one who might... make an impact upon the world." He stared at her, and she returned his gaze, mesmerized. "They are now long dead, and I am not who I once was. If anything, I have come to be the opposite of what they desired. I only hope I've not come to that too late."

Then he stopped, and as if released from a spell, Talina stared at surroundings she hadn't been paying attention to as they walked. They stood in the Hall of the Elders. Directly before them was the seat of the Eldest. Above it, on the rear wall, a story Talina had not noticed on her previous visit flowed across the wood. Even now, the wall was less than half-filled, but she would have sworn it had been unadorned during her previous audience.

"Some stories," he said in a musing voice, "deserve a place of honor among us... and what story is more important than yours?"

Her eyes widened, and she looked over a strip of images clearly depicting the events of Winternight culminating in her flight from those terrible northern mountains.

"So you believe me?" She turned to him almost desperately, searching his face, hope surging within her.

Cain snorted in derision. "Even before you came staggering in the great doors, half dead, those with any sensitivity knew the darkness was on the move. Your words gave definition and shape to what we already knew."

He shook his head impatiently and pointed to the last picture. "And, to the point, *that* is what I brought you here to see!"

Talina gasped softly. "That's Ciaran... but what—who's behind him?"

When her gaze returned to his face, Cain was staring at her intently. "It is exactly who you suspect it to be. Your brother is not entirely himself of late." He paused, as if considering, then continued, "I showed you this to reinforce your already impressive resolve... and there is something else I believe I must tell you. If your brother succeeds in his current aims, our people will surely be shattered and dispossessed, even as we were before the Regathering." There was such a note of finality in his voice that Talina shivered despite herself.

"And if he fails?" she asked.

"For a while, we may have no Eldest at all. Times may be difficult." Cain paused in thought, then shrugged. "No. Times will certainly be far worse than difficult, but our people will survive." His eyes gleamed and he cocked his head. "Tell me, would it be better, do you suppose, to be exiled, leaderless and without hope? Or would you choose to have our people destroyed, bit by bit, more surely than if we had never been?" He looked almost sad, but somehow amused at the same time. It was, it seemed, a common expression for him to wear.

Talina considered for a long time, then frowned. "If I had no other choice, I would say it is better to fight to the end and be destroyed. If we are scattered and given to the chaos once more, we lose what makes us Aylves. We are destroyed as surely as if we were killed, one by one, by Sheklah itself. Such a life would be far worse than never having been at all. Better an honorable end than the non-life we would have otherwise." She looked Cain directly in the eye and said, seriously. "I think I would sooner become a dark elf than choose such an end."

She shook her head as if to dispel the somber atmosphere. "But in the real world... I would choose neither. Neither need become true. We all have a choice, no matter what any prophecy says. It is up to us to change the future. It is not for the future to change us.

"Let that fly in the face of any prophecy—or every prophecy—that has ever been written."

They stood in silence for a moment, then Cain laughed softly. "In some ways, you may be more right than you know. In others, well, you still have time to learn. I feel I must tell you, however, your resolve impresses me, Neyona. And I have not said that in a long time..." The corners of his mouth turned upward in a ghost of a smile. "It has been a very long time indeed." Cain stood silent for another few heartbeats, staring at the wall.

Abruptly then, he turned to her. "Can you find your way back to your rooms? Would that I could speak with you longer, but I have much to do, so I must bid you goodnight."

Talina half bowed, bending her head low in a fashion she knew had not been used in thousands of turnings, before mustering the best of the Old Tongue she could remember. "I e'moinea duo ydra fera, Niyone."

He returned her bow, his own much lower, and as she turned and walked away Talina heard him chuckling behind her in what sounded like anticipation.

10.

It took a full day for Talina to regain her composure enough to face her brother. It was the last thing she wanted to do, but she felt she had no choice. After what Cain had shown her, there was no doubt that she had to stop Ciaran. She didn't know how Lorindar might be influencing her brother, but Ciaran certainly couldn't know whose side he had taken, could he?

She knew where he was staying—as the Elder for clan Anisa, he had immediately moved into In'Kalith's former quarters in the Council Tree. He was actually below her own room. The elves gave their Elders space as close to the ground floor as possible, out of consideration for those who were older and more feeble.

Every step Talina had taken toward Ciaran's quarters added to her trepidation. She had never imagined he would go so far as to stand for Elder without talking to her, much less try to humiliate her in front of the entire clan. His accusations against her were downright strange, and groundless as far as she could tell. She wasn't even certain whether he would speak with her, now.

She stood before his door for what felt like a very long

time, steeling herself, before she finally knocked.

When he answered the door, Ciaran was in a good mood—until he saw Talina. She watched his expression change from jovial and relaxed to dismayed and angry, then finally settle into wary hostility. Nor did he greet her. Instead, he stared imperiously, waiting for her to speak.

"Cee, can I come in? There are... things we should talk about."

"Oh now you want to talk?!" Ciaran scowled. "After you tried to steal the eldership from me? You've been away for hundreds of turnings, Talina, and you couldn't even talk with me before you tried to keep me from my rightful position!"

Talina stared at him, shocked again despite herself as he continued. "At first, I didn't want to believe it..." Ciaran shook his head. "... Especially as you were hurt, but then came your insane stories, and after that you *did* try to steal the position. He was right. I should have..." Ciaran bit off his sentence, angrily.

Talina's eyes narrowed. "He who, Ciaran? Who was right?"

Ciaran looked away instinctively. "You wouldn't understand."

"Oh?" Talina folded her arms over her chest. "I might understand more than you think. I'm surprised—shocked, actually—that you would deal with Lorindar of all people, but I *understand* more about what's going on than you do, Ciaran."

He stared at her, and for a moment Talina thought she might have a chance, but then he shook his head again. "You *don't* understand. You don't know him at all."

"I know he killed grandfather." Talina looked down,

remembering. "He came for me in my dreams and In'Kalith saved me. It cost him his life."

She looked back up, staring him right in the eye. "Besides, Ciaran, he's been exiled! Even talking to him is forbidden, and for good reason. He's allied himself with Sheklah!"

Ciaran rolled his eyes. "There you go again with your fairytale nonsense. He said you would try something like this, and that we had to stop you at all costs. He's worked too hard, for too long. All he wants is to be reinstated and you came back just to mess things up.

"But you forgot one thing, Talina. You've gotten so caught up in your world-traveling that you think we're backward and ignorant, and we're not. We're not the credulous fools you think we are. If you needed an excuse to be chosen as Elder, you should have at least picked a believable one."

Talina groaned aloud in frustration. "Ciaran, I'll never *be* an Elder! In'Kalith prophesied as much. I have no desire for power. All I'm interested in is the truth... and keeping my flesh and blood from conspiring with Lorindar!"

Ciaran laughed. "Your flesh and blood... you mean you don't know?" He shook his head, pityingly. "Lorindar *IS* our flesh and blood, Talina... He's our great-grandfather, and I know him far better than I know you."

Talina stared at him, dumbstruck, and Ciaran snorted in derision. "As for the exile, you don't understand anything at *all*. Lorindar had more power than the council was comfortable with after the Regathering. His exile was nothing more than politics and now he's finally laid the groundwork to rejoin society!"

Talina repeated slowly. "He killed In'Kalith, Ciaran.

That was *after* he sent an assassin to kill me... and he probably killed our family too!"

Ciaran's eyes were flinty. "I never tried to kill you. I was trying to scare you away... It was our best chance. And he swore he had nothing to do with the rest of the family's death. Unlike *you*, everything he's said has been proven right. I have no reason to disbelieve him. Our *family* has enemies you know nothing about. There are still plenty of people who want to stop him with all the reason in the world to kill our parents! I'm sorry you got caught up in it."

Talina gaped at him. "That was... you?"

Ciaran squirmed a little beneath her hurt, but he set his jaw. "And based on what you've done since then, it was justified, wasn't it? I wish I'd..." He stopped again, then shook his head, this time with finality. "Your plans have been foiled, Talina. I'm glad you're still alive, but you should probably just leave the Talonwood. Our people don't need you to save them." He turned away and closed his door in Talina's face, leaving her gaping after him.

11.

Talina stood in the branches of a talonwood tree overlooking the Aeth. It had been three long days since her brother became Anisa's Elder. That made three days of being stared at or snubbed, or worse, being pointedly ignored by those around her.

Sadly, her own clan was worse than any of the others in that regard, though the tales spread rapidly. The worst of the rumors said *she* had murdered her own family. Talina didn't know where those originated, but it was amazing how much it hurt her to actually have a mother pull a child from her sight because of who she was.

Even a portion of the council seemed to have bought into the idea. They had no proof, of course, so the worst they could do was ignore her. Those who believed her version of the story pretended nothing was wrong, though when they thought she couldn't see, they would seem either sad or bemused by the way things had turned out.

For the most part, people avoided her. If she spoke to them, most would answer, but hurriedly and with gazes averted.

There were a few who pointedly disdained, and even seemed angered by, everyone else's attitude. She couldn't help keeping a mental list of them as the days passed. There were certainly few enough to count.

Cain had visited her twice more to talk at length about what happened during her journeys, and Janrae had made a point of stopping her once more when she stepped outside to feel the air.

Despite those bright spots, the time had been difficult. It didn't seem to be getting any better, either. Talina shook her head, full of disgust and frustration so thick they made her feel physically ill.

Today, the council would publicly announce who had been raised to the position of Eldest, and the crowd around the Aeth stretched back from the clearing all the way into the trees on the three sides that would allow them a view of the ceremony.

Traditionally, the council elected one of their number to the position privately, usually the oldest or acknowledged wisest. In this case, the choice was unclear.

I'Nakima, both longest-serving and wisest of the council members, had declared herself unwilling to take the post and completely recused herself from the process without explanation. That left only twelve to complete the choice and elevate a new Eldest, and with I'Nakima holding herself apart, Ciaran had at least as much chance as any of the others.

Talina still had trouble believing Anisa had selected him as their Elder. If she had become one of the council, the position of Eldest would fall to her simply because of her family lineage. Ciaran wasn't a wise choice, but events of late had proven to her that even the elves could be blinded to the truth if they were unwilling to see.

If that was to be the result, she would stand against it. She must.

Would she have cared so much had Ciaran not admitted he was conspiring with Lorindar? Somehow, she thought she would, if only from pure stubbornness, but now? There was no question at all. She would stop Ciaran, no matter what it took.

The question was, who had the Elders chosen? Would she even have to speak? She hoped not. She had enough trouble as it was. All she wanted was to leave once more—to return to the wandering that had consumed so much of her life.

She couldn't do that.

A ripple went through the crowd below as the Elders approached, and it parted, a path opening through it almost like a tear in the very fabric of her people. Down that rent strode the thirteen Elders, two abreast with I'Nakima at their head. They were all dressed in their ceremonial robes of office, with finely-wrought rapiers at their sides. Ciaran was in the rearmost pair, head held high, staring straight ahead. From her position above and behind them, Talina couldn't see much, but the tilt of his head and the straightness of his bearing were obvious, and her heart seemed to stop. He'd done it. She'd no doubt now. She knew him too well. The only question was what she could possibly say to make them all see the truth. Based on her recent conversation with her brother, the answer to that question was a grim one.

I'Nakima raised her hands for silence, and a hush fell over those assembled below. Talina knew that in her grandfather's lifetime, a new Eldest had been chosen only four times, and of those, I'Nakima had been an Elder for only one of them.

Talina wondered what she was thinking and, most of all, what could have made her remove herself from the selection process for Eldest... Then again, if Ciaran knew about Lorindar, surely I'Nakima did as well.

Whatever the case, her voice was clear and strong as it rang out across the Aeth, beginning the ritual that traditionally marked the selection of Eldest. "De'Ayaia ey cathena, noria le'breala coneya i stiye onya fera hoenia. Fera'de'u son malase cariya onya, pisa ni i piseya tenso e'honin." *To the People let it be known, the time of choosing has come. Before us stands the chosen. Lest there be any dissention among us, look upon him and see him fit for his office.*

I'Nakima began to step aside, clearing the way for Ciaran to come forward before the assembly, but Talina felt her resolve beginning to waver. She could wait no longer. Before either I'Nakima or Ciaran could move to take their traditional places, she cried out, "No!"

Talina hadn't been certain whether she would be heard or not, even from her perch in the branches of the great tree, facing the monolith of the Aeth. All elves knew that as the Aeth had grown from the earth (or had been created by magic, some said) it became a natural amphitheatre. The shape of the stone behind and above the Elders' position turned the entire glade into a great auditorium, but the nature of the auditorium also created a pocket of "dead air" that effectively muffled sound coming from places other than the stage.

Talina had spent much of the previous night testing various locations, trying to find some way to make herself heard as well. Her current position was the only one she'd tested that took advantage of the same dynamics, and she hadn't been certain it would be enough.

The crowd below heard her. Some of them turned to stare, and she called out once more, her heart breaking inside her, "No! It must not be!"

The words she had prepared seemed inadequate, but she was committed now. She cried out as loudly as she was able. "In the memory of all the leaders of the People, and in the sight of the King himself—my brother must never be the Eldest of the Talonwood!"

It was as if a bolt of lightning had struck among them. The assembly was silenced in shock. In living memory, no one had ever challenged the Choosing. It was true, the ceremony called for any in opposition to speak. The phrase, *'Look upon him and see him fit for his office'* was by its very nature such a call, but such a challenge had never been made before. By long tradition, all opposition was dealt with before, not during, the ceremony.

The entire assembly stood as if holding their breaths, and for a moment it seemed that I'Nakima might speak. Before she could, Ciaran stepped forward, brushing her aside with his shoulder, and raised an accusing finger to point across the clearing.

His voice was shaking with suppressed fury as he addressed her. She could hear him clearly, of course, though she was still standing in the branches of the talonwood. "Be silent, you... you traitor!" Anger made his voice rough. "The time for opposition has passed. For all your jealousy, I would never have thought even you would stoop so low! Go back to the Council Tree and bring no further shame on our family. I will deal with you later."

Talina stood silent, gathering herself. She had only one avenue left—one opportunity to stop him, and her gut was a solid knot as she spoke, almost in a whisper. Somehow, her voice still carried clearly across the Aeth, and the entire assembly heard her. "I claim the right of Il'Andama."

12.

If the Aeth had been silent before, now it was deathly still. Il'Andama had never before been invoked in such a setting. It was, at worst, an excuse for revenge. At best, it was a call for redress that came exclusively in council, when an elf stood before the judgment.

At its core, Il'Andama was simply a trial by combat. In the modern day, most found the notion barbaric, and there had been a number of attempts to abolish the law that governed it. Il'Andama was one of the few leftovers from a more dangerous time in her people's history. If the challenged could not produce proof to convince the majority of those present they were not guilty of the crime for which they were accused, the accuser could demand single combat to satisfy the wrong.

The silence lasted for what seemed turnings before Ciaran spoke. "Think what you do, Talina. You know that I would never have…"

Talina's voice cut across his, sounding harsher in her own ears than she would have believed possible. "That you would kill our family? I *HOPE* that was still beyond you. What you've done is, if anything, worse. I charge that you, Ciaran of tribe Anisa, have consorted with Lorindar, the exiled, and with his master, Sheklah, the Defiler. I charge that you have used influence granted by those powers to attain the council position you currently hold, and that you now attempt to use that same influence to gain the position of Eldest.

"You have wronged not only me, brother, but our entire family. In'Kalith, our grandfather, was killed by the same Lorindar with whom you consort. I witnessed it myself in the dream."

Ciaran's face twisted, at first in shock, then in anger and hatred. "You jealous…! Conniving…!" Words seemed to fail him as his mouth worked. Then he stopped. "Very well. These charges are… insane. I can hardly respond to them at all, much less with proof."

Talina's lips tightened. His showmanship never faltered. She had to give him that.

Well, she thought, two could play at that game.

When she prepared for this day, she had brought the same staff that carried her to Estaria as well as a rope, and a few other supplies. She had tied her line to the branch upon which she perched, thinking to slide down to the ground when the time came. It was time, and she began to reach for it, but something stopped her. She had never before felt the confidence that welled up in her, and what she contemplated was insane, but she didn't stop to think. Grabbing her staff—the same one she had used to defend herself from the Helthria, what felt like a lifetime ago—she dropped toward the ground an impossible distance below.

None of those present could be quite sure afterward whether their eyes had deceived them, if the girl leapt from the branches of the great tree, landing in a crouch far, far below, or whether she was simply above, then magically appeared on the ground. Whatever happened, it was not the impossibly sudden change in position that caught the crowd's attention, but a sudden sense of power that surrounded her. How they perceived it, few could have described, and those few were the oldest and most learned of the sages. However it existed, it was as real as the sun, the grass and the great talonwoods themselves, and vast as the forest in which they stood.

After crouching with her eyes closed, Talina drew herself slowly to her feet, then opened her mouth to speak. In hardly a moment, though, she closed it again. The time for speaking was over, and instead she stepped forward, raising her staff before her.

Ciaran drew his sword and the crowd between them parted. His face hardened into an emotionless mask as he strode toward her.

She too began to move, and time became surreal as they crossed the Aeth toward each other. It was a shock when Ciaran's hand blurred and his sword struck for her head. Almost before he moved, her staff was in place to block him, then twisting to strike.

Talina had long trained with the staff, but only in self-defense. She was no warrior. Il'Andama had been a terrible choice. She knew that before she offered the challenge.

It didn't matter. Terrible as it might be, it was the only option she had left. Nothing else she could think of would allow her to interpose herself between her brother and the headship of the council.

At first he was cautious, feeling her out. She blocked his first two attacks, attempted a strike and failed.

Ciaran sneered, "You're slow, Talina. You've been gone for too long. You're a stranger to your own people!" He was right. She seemed clumsy, even to herself, and he had her on the defensive already.

Ciaran exerted himself, and it only took a few more strikes before he was literally fighting circles around her. As he circled, he grated, "Admit it, sister. Your only motivation—your *true* motivation—is nothing more than jealousy! I have rightfully gained the position you wished for yourself!"

They both knew he could have killed her at will, but his fury was firmly under control now. He wanted nothing so much as to humiliate her in front of the entire assembly.

Ciaran began hacking at her staff, as if it were a tree trunk, cutting notches in it. Catching the alarmed look on her face, he sneered and redoubled his efforts. Wood chips sprayed out from them with every blow, and Talina realized he was going to disarm her.

Ciaran's face broke into a vicious grin. "Tell me, how would it even be possible to disprove such charges as you've laid?" He tilted his head. "If you admit what you've done, I will still let you live."

Talina knew it would only take a few more strikes... A particularly strong swing broke her staff in half and she instinctively reared back and threw it at him, following up with a kick that should have sent him reeling.

He dodged instead, and he was done toying with her.

His sword came down in an overhead arc that was meant to kill.

13.

Talina fell backward, raising her hands above her to block his blow with... her staff? There was no time for confusion. There was indeed a staff in her hands. She twisted her body and shoved against Ciaran's blade with everything she could muster and he stumbled sideways, knocked off balance.

Talina rose to her feet once more, advancing now, and the staff she had somehow gained seemed a living thing in her hands. A skill she hadn't thought she possessed flowed through her, and she found she could now meet her brother blow for blow.

His sword came at her ribs. She moved to block, jerked out of the way at the last second, and parried.

Strike, dodge, strike, dodge, block, parry...

"I have no wish to kill you, Ciaran." Talina's own words rang across the assembly like a smith's hammer against hot iron.

Neither combatant seemed aware, but as the fight continued, their speed gradually increased until they were a blur, neither one losing even a blow to the other.

Ciaran's mouth distorted in a snarl, and his eyes actually glowed as he allowed fury and... something else to drive him on, questing, seeking, looking for an opening.

"You must not lead the Aylves into darkness! I won't allow it!" Talina's voice grated as she strained to keep up the pace.

Strike, block, strike, parry, dodge, strike...

Though she could now match Ciaran through means she only dimly understood, Talina still didn't have an advantage. He never left her an opening, and she began to tire quickly.

Talina realized she must do something, anything, to break their combat. He was in better condition than she was. It was a matter of time—probably not much time—before she missed a crucial block.

Block, strike, block, block, strike, block...

"Yield, brother! For the sake of our people and In'Kalith's memory! I beg you!" Talina was panting now with exertion.

She began to respond a bit more slowly to each blow, measuring her strikes. Soon she was acting purely on the defensive, and she saw Ciaran's face twist in triumph as he redoubled his efforts, panting as well.

It took every bit of skill and timing she could muster to allow herself to block by smaller and smaller margins, waiting for an opening. Then came the strike she'd been hoping for—Ciaran overextended himself.

Talina lashed out with all the speed she had feigned losing. Instead of trying to block the thrust, the only possible choice if she had truly been tiring, Talina wrenched herself to the right, swinging for Ciaran's chest with the tip of her staff.

Instantly, she knew she had misjudged. She HAD been tiring, and her pretense had hidden it even from her. It had been an awkward blow, its clumsiness made worse by her own fatigue, and it forced her within Ciaran's reach to carry it through. As she felt her staff connect with his torso, his rapier struck into her side, burying itself in her flesh.

Her blow, too, landed. Where Ciaran's weapon was built to pierce, hers was made for smashing, and she hit near the center of his chest. Talina heard bone snap under her blow, and Ciaran fell back, losing hold of his sword.

Both reacted as quickly as their depleted strength allowed. Ciaran scrambled madly for his weapon, while Talina twisted, crying out at the sword still stuck into her, and brought the butt of her staff around to take him in the side of the head.

She could have killed him with that stroke. He had fixated on regaining his weapon, and Talina saw it coming.

She thought she had been prepared to kill him—had steeled herself for it—but when she had the opportunity, it was beyond her. Instead, Talina put less than her full strength into the strike, knocking Ciaran unconscious.

As he fell, Talina's strength, too, failed, and she stood, swaying above him, leaning on the staff she still hadn't had time to look at properly. With trembling fingers, she reached down and placed her hand on the hilt of the sword, which remained buried in her side.

The foreign object in her flesh was too much to endure. Talina slid the thin blade free and pain smashed into her like a hammer blow. She gasped and nearly fell, but holding tight to her staff saved her once more.

It was then, with her blood staining her side, holding her brother's sword, still wet from her own wound, that she heard the crowd.

It took a moment for her to comprehend their cries and pull herself from her daze of exhaustion enough to turn toward the forest behind her, away from the Aeth.

What she saw was a scene from a nightmare. A dozen Helthria rampaged through the crowd, their teeth and claws glinting impossibly white in the sun—except where they were stained red with the blood of her people. As the assembly attempted to scatter, screaming in panic, the beasts tore their way through whatever lay in their paths.

I'Nakima was crying out in a commanding voice, trying frantically to clear her people out of the monsters' way, but Talina couldn't tell whether anyone even heard over the bedlam.

It was simply too much. Somehow, impossibly, she had defeated her brother. By Aylvish law, she'd proved her case. *Wasn't that enough?*

Her question was foolish. The enemy didn't care about what was fair.

As if to prove her point, Talina watched one of the scorpion cats crush a man's chest with one paw. She felt desperation rising within her, as she had at her family's home many long days before. This time, however, instead of sorrow and despair, she was filled with rage.

Dropping her brother's sword and raising the staff in her hand, Talina cried out in fury, once again only distantly aware of her own words. "Vilana! Fera son sidu con an cathnos il alka Il'Feron! Madradaria cariya onya tesas! Ey'u manese tarioso eyam! Bicole onar Ayaia!"

Falling silent even as she noted that all the creatures were headed straight for her, Talina summoned every bit of power within her and, hoping her magic would DO something for once, flung it at the nearest beast. She had no idea what to expect, but she needed to act.

She felt the staff in her hand resonate strangely, echoing her fury. Then, from within the creature's fur, something pierced its skin, growing into it and reaching living tendrils for the ground. With her mind sluggish from blood loss and fatigue, it took several heartbeats for Talina to realize the growths must have come from some kind of seed, caught in the Helthria's coat. The creature crouched for another leap forward and the tendrils took root, jerking it violently to a stop. Multiple other growths followed, reaching down from its limbs and body to anchor themselves in the ground. The monster stood there for an instant, quivering against its newly grown bonds. Then, it collapsed. The progress from that point was too rapid to follow. Before her eyes, living plant matter consumed it, pulling it into the ground and enveloping it.

For an instant, Talina simply froze, staring at the spot where the Helthria had disappeared. The pain in her side and her exhaustion dragged at her, but there was no time. She shook off her shock, adrenaline giving her strength as she turned to give another beast the same treatment. This time only one living shackle awoke. A single seed had been caught in its fur, and when it sprouted, the resulting shoot anchored the beast to the ground by a paw. As it struggled there, throwing itself violently to and fro, Talina watched a rope of plant matter grow up around its leg and into its flesh, then break downward through its belly to send another root into the ground beneath, jerking it down.

Four others were nearly upon her now, finally clearing the crowd, and Talina felt drained by her second effort. As she turned to a third monster, raising her staff, a roar rang from above and behind her, on the great monoliths of the Aeth. Talina didn't look around, instead hurling her magic at the beast bearing down on her.

Pushing herself on by mere force of will, she turned to the fourth without waiting to see what happened. If she were to die, it would be defending her people. She would never give up, even to the last instant.

Talina loosed her magic at the fourth and feebly began to raise her staff to the fifth, but knew even before she turned that it was too late. It was simply too close, and she was too weak.

Then, in her mind, a voice howled, *DOWN, TALAN!* Before she could even think to respond, something slammed into her back, driving her to her belly on the ground, and above her she heard a terrific roar. She couldn't see what it was. The fall had stunned her, and even if it hadn't, she was too weak to move. The pain and exertion, not to mention the repeated shocks, were finally catching up with her. Through the tiny window of vision she had left, Talina saw the Helthria, stopped in their tracks.

Now only distantly aware, Talina saw them begin to circle, one passing out of her sight. Then the one she could still see leapt toward her once more, only to be struck by a huge white paw that swatted it aside like a toy. There was a snarl behind her and the sound of something striking the ground, followed by a crunch and a squeal of pain.

The last thing Talina felt before she passed out was something rough licking at her side where the wound from

Ciaran's sword still bled. Distantly, with a sense of awe, Talina realized what stood above her.

14.

Talina floated in and out of wakefulness at irregular intervals for an indeterminable time. Her thoughts were muddled. All-too-real visions of monsters tearing her to pieces interwove with voices that might have been real.

"... Barely alive." Her consciousness was a muddled mess. Reality blurred. It could have been a second or an hour before the next words. "Sleeping... Don't disturb..." There was a low growl.

Talina tried to open her eyes... to speak... but it was too much effort, and darkness took her again.

Eventually, finally, she fell into a dreamless sleep.

When Talina awoke, she tried to sit up, startled to consciousness by... something. Her side was an instant mass of agony, and she fell back to the mattress, gritting her teeth.

Beside the bed she heard a snort. As she looked around, a huge feline face appeared before her. It was sleek and white, and a long mane flowed down the creature's neck. She lay once more in her own guest room in the Council Tree, and the wood tones of the walls soothed her in the dim light from the candle that had been left burning on her bedside table.

It took you long enough. The voice spoke directly into her mind as the soft, pink nose went down to nuzzle gingerly at her side. Talina winced. "You're..." She trailed off, her voice so weak as to be inaudible.

I am Santhria. I am Barilan. The huge feline raised his head once more to stare down into her eyes. *Do not speak, Talan. Your strength must recover.*

The Santhria were almost a myth among the Elves. Legend said they had been set as guardians over the Talonwood by the King himself after the Cataclysm, when the first talonwood seedling was given into the Elves' sacred charge. Throughout the Great War, the Santhria were the Talonwood's staunchest defenders, and Warden Ay'Thera had been the last companion one of their number chose to adopt. When she was murdered, they withdrew into the forest, and her people had rarely seen them since.

Barilan was magnificent. His body had the lean savagery and might of a tiger, but he was even larger and bulkier than the biggest tiger ever born, barely fitting his 15-link length into the room at all. There was something preternaturally graceful about him, and she couldn't help but feel a pang of fear at his size and the sheer power of his presence. He was so much larger than the twisted Helthria —themselves long-descended from the Santhria—that there was no real comparison.

What would it take, she wondered, for her to make him angry enough to harm her? Surely if she did, she would be dead in an instant.

Talina felt questions welling up within her, one upon another. She was on the verge of trying to speak again when that mental voice chuckled. *My, my, so many questions. You are confused as a cub.*

Clearing her mind, Talina focused past the pain, trying to crystallize a single idea. *You can hear my thoughts?*

What you do not guard, yes. Barilan thought... or was it sent?

Then, how? How did you come to the Aeth? How did I survive? What happened to my people?

Again, the mental chuckle resounded through her, rich and full in a way that put real sound to shame. *How? Simple. We always attend Il Hoeno, though you may not see us.* He considered her for a moment, then continued. *You survived because I jumped from the great pile of rocks and landed on you before those fisthk could reach you. Though you were doing quite well on your own, for one so injured.* That last arrived with a sense of respect, one warrior's respect for another.

And my people? Her worry must have carried with her own mental voice, for Barilan sighed both mentally and physically, an odd duality to "hear" at once.

Some died. Many are wounded. Numbers? I know not. He blew out a breath. *It was not as bad as it might have looked to you. The fisthk were intent on your death. They spent no extra fury upon your kin. It was only when they got tangled that they did serious harm.* His lips distorted in a snarl and he added derisively, *They got tangled far more than the most inept of the People would have—or did.*

Then it wasn't only you? Talina asked.

There were three of us. Not many, but enough for the

likes of the Helthria. We returned them all to the earth. Sadness tinged his sending. *Even then, a brother was gravely hurt. But that is the way of this broken world. Better to face Tarios le'Cathra in honor than shame.*

Talina's brow knit. *How did they even get close without my people sensing them—or smelling them? They stink like the twisted magic of the north.*

Barilan whuffed. *Only to you, Talan. Such is your gift.* He blew out a breath and looked at her sideways.. *Sleep now. When morning comes, your kin will need you. They would have woken you earlier, but I... discouraged them.* There was obvious satisfaction and a touch of mirth attached to that, and Talina decided it was better not to ask.

There was plenty of time for that later, and she was still desperately tired.

No fear, I will wake you in time.

15.

It seemed only moments before she felt a wet nose prodding her hand and blinked awake once more to find Barilan at her side. He turned to regard her with a steady gaze. *Your people have been trying to wake you again. It would be unwise for me to stop them now. There is much to do in little time.*

Talina tried to sit up but sank back, once more surprised at her own weakness and pain.

A knock sounded upon the door, and it opened slowly to reveal a wary young woman's face. Seeing Talina awake, she started to open the door the rest of the way before her eyes fell on Barilan and she stopped.

"Neyona, the Elder I'Nakima sent me. She wishes to see you."

Talina nodded and made as if to rise, then again fell back. Moving was still beyond her.

"Oh don't worry, Neyona. I'll fetch her." The girl turned and hurried away, and Talina simply lay there, her mind still working to grasp her situation.

A short while later, I'Nakima's face appeared in the crack of the door. "May I?" She began opening the door, then stopped, giving Barilan a wary look until he snorted.

Apparently reassured, I'Nakima proceeded to slip into the room and move to a chair across from the bed, keeping a respectful distance from Barilan, who lay with his head next to Talina on the floor.

"You've slept for quite some time. What do you remember, Talina?"

Talina spoke carefully, with as much strength as she could muster. "Most of it. It's not all clear, but I remember most of it."

I'Nakima paused, then asked gently, "What about the staff? Do you remember what staff you were holding?"

"I didn't have a staff. Ciaran broke it when..." Talina paused, thinking again and remembering. She DID have a staff. It seemed so natural at the time that she hadn't even considered how she got it. It was just there. It took another moment to recall fully, and when she did, Talina gasped. "The Staff of Elders? But..."

I'Nakima nodded wryly. "I fear this may be a less than restful awakening, and..." she hesitated." The reality we face is far harsher than you deserve, especially considering how much you've already given for our people."

Talina grimaced. "That doesn't sound good, but it's not going to get better because you haven't told me."

I'Nakima nodded again. "The People are divided. Some of us—many of us—saw what you did at the Aeth, how you would have given your life for The People, defending us first from... your brother... and then from the Helthria." I'Nakima hesitated, and Talina sensed currents beneath what she was saying that seemed pregnant with deeper meaning, especially the comment about Ciaran.

I'Nakima continued before Talina could get a better read. "Everyone else is falling into a different camp. You knew even before Il Hoeno there were rumors that you had killed the rest of your family." I'Nakima didn't quite flinch at the sudden heat in Talina's eyes, but she could see the Elder's discomfort in her expression. "Now, after what happened, they claim that it was you who called the Helthria down upon us rather than Ciaran or—" her lips curled "—Lorindar."

Talina's jaw dropped open in shock. She recovered, closing it after only a second and shaking her head. "What?! Really?"

I'Nakima nodded gravely. "Yes, and besides that there's the matter of the staff." She fixed her gaze on the staff leaning against the wall by the bed that Talina had unknowingly reached out to touch when I'Nakima broke the news to her. Its very presence carried a haze of intangible power, so much so that touching it would have seemed almost impious to Talina—if it didn't come so naturally.

"We could hardly get you to let it go when we put you to bed, and it... resisted... our efforts to remove it from the room. Some are already claiming that your use of the staff makes you a Warden of the Talonwood." She fixed Talina with a steady gaze. "Others are claiming you stole it and have bound it to you with the same dark magic by which you control the Helthria."

The weight of the statement hovered between them for a few heartbeats, before Talina inhaled sharply. "What do you believe?" Even as she asked the question, Talina found her self-assurance rock solid—she was simply curious what I'Nakima thought. After everything she'd been through, others' opinions—even those of the Elders—held little power over her. Perhaps she should be concerned that so many of her people obviously thought her an agent of the dark, but she could no longer bring herself to care. She knew who she was. That was enough.

I'Nakima laughed musically, "Me? I don't know what to think. I saw those monsters with my own eyes. They were there to destroy you. As for the staff?" She shook her head. "I've no idea, Talina. We have no test for the office of Warden. Ay'Thera was the last, and since then, well..." She spread her hands, half fatalistically and half in sheer helplessness.

Talina stared at her, then asked, slowly, "So, where does that leave us?"

I'Nakima returned Talina's gaze, head cocked to the side, measuring her.

The silence between them stretched out, with I'Nakima making no reply. Talina's discomfort grew as the seconds ticked by, but she didn't let it show on her face. Her gut told her that I'Nakima's response could weigh heavily on her future.

After a full minute, I'Nakima's gaze dropped and the Elder barked out a short, sharp sound that was almost a laugh. "Flee, girl."

Talina blinked in surprise. "Flee? Now?"

I'Nakima nodded sharply. "It is too dangerous for you here. I fear if you stay they will try to take your life."

Talina laughed harshly in return. "If I won't run from Lorindar and the Helthria, why would I run from this? You've mistaken who I am, I'Nakima."

I'Nakima's gaze dropped once more and she sighed. Talina was about to speak when I'Nakima breathed, "Oh to have In'Kalith back..." She looked up into Talina's face once again, then said, flatly, "There are factions at work among our people of which you know nothing. If you stay here, you will become enmeshed in their coils. In'Kalith might have protected you—created a space for you to grow. I cannot."

It was Talina's turn to measure I'Nakima then, and the other Elf couldn't meet her gaze. After another long silence, Talina asked, "What machinations could possibly be more important than the darkness in the north? Show me which of the People refuses to put aside their grudges under that threat. When it comes, Sheklah will make what we faced during the Separation look like a picnic on the terrace."

I'Nakima's eyes were bleak. "Who do you think conspired to *free* the Byzimyanny, girl? Do you really believe we live in such a vacuum? How do you think your brother got his power?"

Talina stared in shock once more and I'Nakima sniffed and nodded, her face showing the edge of something grim and ugly. Was that satisfaction? "That's right, and he's been up and about for days now, telling 'his side' of the story to anyone who will listen.

"If you choose to stay, you will not survive, unless you ally yourself with..." I'Nakima broke off and her lips compressed into a thin line. Then she shook her head once and rose to her feet, turning toward the door. "You have my counsel, Neyona. And now I have much to do."

Talina opened her mouth to call I'Nakima back, but no sound came out. As the Elder left the room, Barilan roused from where he lay next to Talina's bed to stare at her. *I trust* that *one even less than most Ayaia.* His sending carried a strong flavor of disgust, as if he'd taken a bite of something rotten.

Talina looked at him quizzically. *Even less than most? Meaning you don't trust any of us?*

Barilan returned her gaze with a flat stare. *We trust you—now. You proved yourself before the great rocks.* Then, reluctantly, he added, *There are others. A few.*

But why? Talina's puzzlement was plain.

Barilan yawned, showing great white teeth. *Is it not obvious? Your people are a tool of the Madradaria. So it has been since the Betrayer killed the first Talan. For an age, the Santhria have watched the Ayaia pledge yourselves to Il'Feron in word alone and serve the Madradaria with your actions. Few have the integrity of Cathferona. Though redeemed, you are yet corrupt.* Disgust once more flooded his sending and Talina shook her head.

But... Why me? Why come to my aid?

Barilan gave her a sidelong glance, seeming almost resentful. *Because Il'Feron asked... And you are Talan. This is a new thing.*

Talina shook her head, her thoughts whirling. Il'Feron was the King of Yore. The King had asked Barilan to protect her?! And Talan meant Warden of the Talonwood! If that wasn't confirmation enough, nothing could be.

But she was allowing herself to be distracted when she had a decision to make. I'Nakima's warning played back through her mind. She sent, *What do YOU think I should do, Barilan?*

He was silent for a time before letting out a great "Whuffff" of breath. *Stand, sister. Stand and fight.*

Something stirred in Talina's heart at the words and she looked up at him, her expression guarded. You think she's wrong? That I should fight them? Talina's thoughtfulness was tinged with something dark and hungry that even she could feel was dangerous. She wanted to destroy every single being who'd had any part in her family's murder.

Barilan's mental tone carried a shrug. *You are Talan. Whatever ground you claim, we will take it. Whatever path you choose, the Madradaria will be broken. I know your heart, sister. Surrender is not in you. Stand and fight.*

Talina fell silent then, thinking deeply. A hard, stubborn part of her yearned to follow Barilan's advice. Running away went completely against her grain, and I'Nakima's urging to 'flee' only added to that determination. On the other side of the coin, though, she had felt off-balance ever since she came to Estaria. It was as if the city the Aylves had carved into the heart of the Talonwood were the Enemy's own ground, and she had been fighting on their soil.

And if I choose to leave?

Barilan yawned again. When I smell fear in your sweat, I will know it is time to stiffen your spine, sister. *Until that day, you are Talan. Il'Feron trusts your judgment. So shall I.*

A few hours later, Talina paused to look back at Estaria, her side a mass of pain. She sat upon Barilan's broad back, the Staff of Elders across her knees, her mind still in turmoil.

Barilan had been right. Her decision was not based in fear, but in the desire to find healthy ground upon which to grow a proper defense for her people. Some dark corner of her was certain that nothing but fungus would grow upon the rotten heart of the Aylvish empire.

It bothered her—at least a little anyway—what they might think of her for 'running away,' but she knew it was the right thing to do.

If I'Nakima was telling her the truth and her own people were partially responsible for the very threat she had come to rally them against, she had some rethinking to do.

The fact that her own brother had joined the forces of darkness bore no small part in her decision. She needed space to regain her footing. Some of the guilt of Ciaran's actions must, inevitably, be hers to bear as well, for he was her brother. His actions—his betrayal—cut her more deeply and more terribly than his sword had done. She must, in some measure, atone for his wrongs.

Barilan grunted beneath her, sending her a mental objection, and she smiled despite the pain still lancing through her side. If nothing else, she had gained unexpected allies in her battle. Furthermore, the staff across her lap testified to her new office, whatever the other elves believed. She barely knew what it meant to be Warden, even now.

All she could do was press on and trust that the future held better than the past. Or, she would trust that she could bring others into a better world than that in which she, herself, had lived. Wherever hope lay, she must find it, for the way ahead only grew darker.

Epilogue

The elf maid held tightly to the Santhria's mane as the great feline paced up over the crest of the hill. The warden's guardian followed the road leading out of Estaria, barely aware of the weight upon his back. The old man tamped down the tobacco in his pipe and smiled fondly, watching the pair.

Behind him, the dark presence of Lorindar roiled with fury.

The old man paid him no heed, tugging his beard and humming to himself as the vista painted across the great sheet of crystal faded.

"If I could find you, I would *KILL YOU*!" Lorindar's impotence and rage were boiling over, and the shadows around him roiled with their power.

The old man glanced back at him, frowning slightly, and asked, "Do you take any lesson… any at all from the fact that you *cannot* find me? The location of this place is concealed from you, even while your spirit is allowed to visit me. Do you think simple power is all you face? I come and go as I please, yet you have no notion where we are. What does that tell you, Lorindar?"

There was neither challenge nor taunting in the old man's tone, but it pushed the other into incoherent gurgling that trailed off into silence. For a long time, Lorindar simply stared at him, hatred rolling off him in waves.

Real pity filled the old man, and he shook his head. "Even you wished to be my brother once, Lorindar. Do you remember?"

"I remember, old fool. And I discovered in time that I didn't need *you!* I found my power elsewhere. The dark master was willing to give when your lord was not! You *LOST ME*, old man."

The old man turned to gaze steadily into the cowl where Lorindar's red eyes glowed. "Your heart was found wanting. For that reason, you were denied the staff... And so, here we are."

He puffed his pipe for a moment, then added. "Even your knee will bow one day, Lorindar."

Contempt filled the other's grating, hateful voice. "I would cease to exist, first!"

The old man simply shrugged. "Self-destruction is your prerogative, but bow you will, regardless."

Lorindar scoffed, "Your king has put the scepter of rulership into the hands of the mortals, old fool. My master will shatter time and reduce you to a state worse than death! I will have that staff as a trophy. I want nothing of its power."

The old man nodded, but his tone finally held a hint of mockery when he replied. "Yes. And a fine start you've made of the whole business, haven't you?"

In trouble, though she faltered,
the King would hear her call,
In darkness, though she lost her way,
he never let her fall.
Let no man doubt the justice
in the wounded heart she bore,
For it alone might carry through
to win the demons' war.

Character Roster

Aolaira [Ow-lay-ruh]: Talina's horse

Aratan [Eh-ruh-tan]: Bretran's half-brother

> *Race* - Deegani

> *History* - Son of the King of Degan, in succession for the throne of Degan.

> *Allegiance* - Unknown

Ay'Thera [Eye-they-ruh]: The Warden of the Talonwood

> *Race* - Aylf

> *History* - Murdered by a traitor at the end of the Great War after successfully leading her people against Sheklah.

> *Allegiance* - King of Yore

Barilan [Bah-ri-lawn]: A guardian of the Aeth Al'Miera who adopts Talina

> *Race* - Santhria

> *History* - Unspecified

> *Allegiance* - King of Yore

Byzimyanny [Buy-zim-yannee]: Term used by the Aylves to refer to Sheklah. (See Sheklah)

Bretran [Bre-tran]: Primary companion of Lady Talina of the Aylves, Speculation: May be the "Scion of Watchmen Bright" in the prophecies of Eschaton.

Race - Deegani

History - Son of the King of Degan, in succession for the throne of Degan.

Allegiance - King of Yore

Cain [Kayn]: The Keeper of the Histories for the Aylves, responsible for recording their histories in the Council Tree.

Race - Aylf

History - Unknown

Allegiance - King of Yore

Calista [Kal-liss-tuh]: A close friend of Ciaran. A member of clan Garik.

Race - Aylf

History - Grew up in the capital in the circle surrounding the elves' council and court.

Allegiance - Unknown, presumably Lorindar.

Ciaran [See-ah-run]: Talina's youngest brother. A member of clan Anisa.

Race - Aylf

History - Grew up with Talina a few days' travel from Estaria, daughter of Kalin

Allegiance - Unknown, presumably Lorindar.

Estella [Ess-tell-luh]: Talina's sister. A member of clan Anisa.

Race - Aylf

History - Grew up with Talina a few days' travel from Estaria, daughter of Kalin.

Allegiance - Unknown

Great Wizard of Yore [Grate-Wizerd]: Liegeman of the King of Yore, Major figure in the history of Eschaton.

> *Race* - Unknown

> *History* - Conflicting reports as to origin. Defeated Sheklah, the nameless, in the Battle of Ages.

> *Allegiance* - King of Yore

Il'Feron [Ill-feh-roan]: (See for King of Yore)

I'Nakima [Ee-naw-kee-maw]: A member of clan Garik

> *Race* - Aylf

> *History* – Long-time elder of clan Garik and member of the elvish council.

> *Allegiance* - Unknown

In'Kalith [In-kalith]: Talina's grandfather, Eldest of the Talonwood. A member of clan Anisa.

> *Race* - Aylf

> *History* - Son of the exiled Lorindar, later raised to Eldest of the Talonwood.

> *Allegiance* - King of Yore

In'Lokrim [In-low-krim]: Talina's ancestor, Eldest of the Talonwood. A member of clan Anisa.

> *Race* - Aylf

> *History* - Unknown

> *Allegiance* - King of Yore

Janrae [Jan-ray]: A member of clan Orlon who has all-but declared allegiance to Talina.

> *Race* - Aylf

> *History* - A trader and merchant who had dealings with Talina's father.

> *Allegiance* – Unknown, Presumably King of Yore

King of Yore [King-Uv-Yor]: The ruler of the world in the time before Sheklah and the Battle of Ages.

> *Race* - Unknown

> *History* - Unknown

> *Also known as:* Il'Feron (Elves)

Licia [Liss-ee-yuh]: A healer who presumably cared for Talina. A member of clan Strovina

> *Race* - Aylf

> *History* - Grew up in the city of Estaria to parents who served the elvish council.

> *Allegiance* - Unknown

Lorindar [Low-rhin-darr]: A member of clan Anisa who attempted to kill Talina multiple times, did kill her grandfather In'Kalith and very likely was also responsible for the death of her family.

> *Race* - Aylf

> *History* - Grandfather of Talina, father of In'Kalith. Exiled shortly after the Regathering for unknown reasons.

> *Allegiance* - Sheklah

Malakai [Ma-la-kye]: Companion of Cyrith, also liegeman and messenger to the King of Yore.

> *Race* - Deegani (Presumed)

> *History* - Presumably raised (or at least sheltered by) the Fae. Unusual for a Deegani.

> *Allegiance* - King of Yore

Nameless One [Naym-less Won]: Term used by the Deegani to refer to Sheklah. (See Sheklah)

N'Ahlren [N-awl-ruhn]: Head of the largest family in clan Anisa.

> *Race* - Aylf

> *History* - Raised in a remote part of the Talonwood.

> *Allegiance* - Unknown

Sestan [Sess-tuhn]: A close friend of Ciaran. A member of clan Garik. Grandson of I'Nakima.

> *Race* - Aylf

> *History* - Raised in the Elvish court surrounded by political intrigue.

> *Allegiance* - Unknown, presumably Lorindar.

Sheklah [Shek-law]: The proper name of the evil being who rose up in opposition to the King of Yore in the age of Yore.

> *Race* - Unknown

> *History* - Conflicting reports as to origin. Lost to the Great Wizard of Yore in the Battle of Ages. Was presumably imprisoned in the northern mountains (the Madra'risa) thereafter.

> *Allegiance* - Unknown

Talina [Ta-lee-nuh]: Speculation: May be the "Princess of the Woodlands" referred to in the prophecies of Eschaton. Confirmed to be a Warden of the Talonwood by her use of the Staff of Elders and the testimony of Barilan, the Santhria guardian.

> *Race* - Aylf

> *History* - World traveler. Assured by her grandfather that she would never be an Elder of the Talonwood.

> *Allegiance* - King of Yore

Glossary

Aeth al'Miera le'Bicola [ayth al-me-ruh lay-bee-co-luh]: The Glade of the Ancient Guardians—the elves most sacred and revered site, used for important ceremonies.

Anisa [Uh-nee-suh]: Elvish clan, generally revered for leadership and world knowledge.

Ayaia [eye-ay-yuh]: Original name for the Elves, from the Old Tongue.

Aylves [Ale-vz]: One of the seven races of men. Long-lived, but slow to reproduce. Family-based, clannish society.

> *Also known as:* Elves (commonly)

Battle of Ages [Bad-dle uv Ajes]: The battle waged long ago between the Great Wizard and Sheklah the Nameless that resulted in Sheklah's defeat and presumable imprisonment.

Cataclysm [Cat-uh-cli-zum]: The ancient event that divided both the land of Eschaton and its people, originally the great Sidhe, into the seven races of men.

Changer [Chain-jer]: One of the seven races of men. Able to shape-shift into other forms, such as (commonly) wolves.

Also known as: Half-men, Were-men, etc.

Council [Cown-sill]: The ruling body of the Aylvish people.

Council Tree [Cown-sill Tree]: The seat of the council that rules the Aylvish people and symbol of the Aylves among other races.

Daemons [Day-muns]: Magical beings that once originated as Engyls, now twisted to the service of their master, Sheklah.

Degan [Day-gon]: One of the seven races of men. Short-lived, industrious and fecund. Tend toward feudal or imperial political structures. Plural: Deegani [Day-gon-ee]

Also -- The primary political unit of the race of Degan, an empire.

Elder [El-dur]: A member of the elvish council and judge for disputes among the clan to which he or she belongs.

Eldest [El-dust]: The leader of the elvish council and effective leader of the elvish race.

Elf [Elf]: (See Aylves)

Engyl [En-gill]: A magical being, often tasked with the oversight of elemental forces. Possessing free will and often great intelligence and power. Usually bound to a particular area.

Eschaton [Es-ka-tawn]: The world upon which the events of Winternight take place.

Estaria [Es-tar-ee-yuh]: The only city ever constructed by the Elves and seat of their government.

Fisthk [Fisthkuh]: Literally, poop. (Old Tongue)

Fae [Fay]: One of the seven races of men. Most known for digging and underground exploration. Tend toward dynastic or familial political structures (extended clans).

Also known as: Fair Folk, Dwarves, Fairies

Great Oath [Grayt Ohth]: A direct magical binding mysteriously connected with the forces of creation. Those who swear by it are bound beyond their ability to resist. (See Old Magic.)

Garik Clan [Geh-rick Clan]: Elvish clan, generally known for agriculture and (comparative) fertility.

The Great War [Duh Grate Wor]: The war in which Sheklah faced the King of Yore and lost several thousand turnings ago.

Gygans [Guy-gans]: One of the seven races of men. Most known for their great size and passion for creating megalithic structures. Tend toward democratic or republican political structures.

Also known as: Giants

Helthria [Hell-three-yuh]: A demonic perversion of the Santhria created by Sheklah during the Great War.

Il'Andama [Ill An-daw-maw]: Ancient rite of trial by combat used by the Elves as a court of last resort.

Links [Linkz]: A unit of measurement (somewhat less than a foot).

Madradaria [Mah-draw-daw-ree-uh]: The enemies of the King of Yore, generally headed by and including Sheklah.

Madra'risa **[Mah-draw-ree-suh]:** The black mountains of The North (See North, the) under which Sheklah the nameless was long thought to be imprisoned.

Neyona [Nay-yo-nuh]: Old Tongue term translated "my lady"

Niyone [Nee-yown]: Old Tongue term translated "my lord"

North, the [North]: The area traditionally held to be the original domain of Sheklah, now covered in mostly-uninhabited dark forests.

The Old Tongue [Thee Ohld Tung]: The language used by the Elves before the modern tongue that they adopted from surrounding races.

Orlon [Or-lawn]: Elvish clan, generally known for industriousness and wealth.

The Great Pogrom [Duh Grate Pog-rawm]: A slaughter of tens of thousands of elves carried out during The Separation by Changers allied to Sheklah.

Prophecies of Eschaton [Praw-fu-seez uv Es-kuh-tawn]: Writings from the Book of Yore that predict the future of Eschaton, including the Reckoning.

Races of Man [Rasus uv Man]: The seven different races descended from the Sidhe, the eighth and original race. See: Aylves, Changers, Deegani, Fae, Gygans, Simianites, and Theurgans

Reckoning [Wreck-un-ing]: Fabled time of judgment, during which the races of man will be united and the King of Yore will return to mete out justice to everyone, great and small.

The Regathering [Duh Ree-Ga-thur-ing]: The time in which the Aylves were regathered from the Separation, just over a thousand turnings ago.

Sage [Sayj]: Advanced elvish magic user and wise one.

Santhria [San-three-yuh]: Great white cats set to guard the Talonwood by the King of Yore.

The Separation [Duh Sep-uh-ray-shun]: A time when the Aylves were dispersed across the face of Eschaton.

Sidhe [She]: The original, unblemished race of man from before the Cataclysm. Characteristics and tendencies only rumored.

Simia [Si-me-uh]: One of the seven races of men. Short-lived, brutish and often considered stupid by the other races. Reproduce VERY quickly. Political tendencies unknown (because they've always been enslaved). Plural: Simianites [Si-me-uh-nites]

Also known as: Trolls

Talan [Taw-lawn]: Talon Warden—a Warden of the Talonwood (Old Tongue)

Talonwood [Taa-lawn-wood]: The forest in which the elves live, the only home to the talonwood trees.

Theurgans [Thur-guns]: One of the seven races of men. Long-lived, reclusive, and power-hungry. Barely able to reproduce. Political tendencies unknown.

Also known as: Wizards

Troll [Trohl]: (See Simia)

Turning [Turn-ing]: A unit of time measurement. Analogous to (but not necessarily equal to) a year.

Watchmen: [Wotsh-mun]: (See Degan)

Were-men [Where men]: (See Changer)

Winternight [Win-tur-night]: A day of power, when all the known magical forces of the world are more active and available.

Yore [Your]: A time from before the Cataclysm, when the world was young, inhabited by the Sidhe and directly governed by the King of Yore.

About the Author

© 2023 - Rachel Collins Photography LLC

Jared N. Michaud is a devoted fiction writer driven by a passion for writing that began before he reached age seven. Influenced by literary giants like C.S. Lewis and Orson Scott Card, he discovered the power of storytelling, and at twelve he began crafting his first novel.

Today, Jared writes from a little house in a little town in Wyoming, where he lives with his wife and seven children. As a Christian with a deep love for the truth and appreciation for the values that underlie Western civilization, he endeavors to create myths that will inspire future generations.

An Ancient Covenant
Mythologia – Book 3

Talina drooped across Barilan's shoulders, her side a mass of fire. "How much further?" she gritted, trying not to wince every time his body shifted.

This was not my idea, cub. His own irritation was apparent, but under control. It was matched by a deep compassion for her own equally-apparent pain—and just as obviously caused by that pain. Telepathic communication did not immediately make everything simpler or easier, as she'd always supposed it must, Talina reflected wryly.

'Hearing' her thought, Barilan actually whuffed in amusement. *Wait until you meet your life-mate, Talan. If you think this is complicated...* The extra motion of his breath jostled her yet again, and she winced, but did her best to focus past it. Annoying Barilan was counterproductive, especially considering that in her exhausted, pain-addled state, he was their eyes and ears as well. If some enemy were to come upon them, it would be Barilan who must choose whether to fight or flee. She would have all she could do just to stay on his back.

Barilan's pure-white coat glistened silver in the early moonlight, falling through the branches above, and even through her pain Talina marveled at the fact that she was actually riding a Santhria. She hadn't even been certain she believed in the legendary creatures as recently as a few days ago. Il Hoeno—the ceremony of choosing for the eldest of the Talonwood—had changed everything. She had fought her brother to stop him from being elevated to the position of eldest, then afterward been forced to defend herself against the monstrous Helinao.

The grave wound she took in the battle had been a small price to pay for victory, though thinking of it as a victory still seemed wrong somehow. She didn't regret the stand she'd taken or the price—any of the prices—she'd paid. She did grieve those of her people who had fallen to the Helinao that day, but even that was a price she could not regret.

What still weighed on her, however, was the choice she had made shortly afterward. Leaving Estaria went against her grain. She'd never been one to run from a fight, and this was a fight for the very soul of her people. Her decision had been driven by the need to find solid footing upon which to carry on the fight. Now she was questioning that logic, driven in no small part by the increasingly-agonizing wound in her side.

Talina wasn't even sure where they were any longer, much less where they were going. She knew they had ridden east out of the Elven city of Estaria, but that was at least two days ago, and her sense of direction was far below its usual keenness. Barilan allowed her to rest briefly each night, but he never did so himself, and he always seemed on edge when he returned to wake her.

They had reached the edge of the Talonwood proper the night before, but Barilan's tension only seemed to increase proportionally as they got farther from Estaria. She had asked him why once or twice without receiving a useful answer. The only sense she got from him telepathically was a brooding watchfulness overlaying tension and ready violence.

Part of Talina hoped he was jumping at shadows, but in her heart she knew he wasn't. Something was wrong, and she had no idea what it might be. There were the Helthria, of course. The giant, venomous mutants were distantly related to Barilan's own people. Even the black-cloaked assassin who tried to end her life when she first returned to the Talonwood and had turned out to be her brother, Ciaran, could be out there.

And those were just the threats she knew about. The other, darker possibilities were so much worse. The Helthria were, or had been, the least of the Nameless One's —no of Sheklah's—creatures. Some of his greater monsters, like the Kelizad or the Draugan, didn't even bear contemplating... but they'd haunted her dreams of late.

That was probably another reason she hadn't slept well, as if her side wasn't enough trouble.

Crack—A branch broke off to their left, and Talina's head whipped around toward the sound, her eyes searching the woods. Talina's heart was instantly racing. She caught a flash of motion, then something jumped across the ghost of a trail they were following. Her head turned in pursuit as it streaked through the forest to their right. Had that been a deer?

Relief was as instantaneous as her fright had been, but it left her sagging against Barilan.

Then she heard him growling and a sick, terrible fear gripped her insides. She turned her head slowly back to where the deer had first appeared, knowing she didn't really want to see whatever must be there.

This time, the creature that loomed out of the darkness from their left looked like an overgrown ape. Cascades of hair flowed down its back and dangled like sick strings of seaweed from its arms and chin, and the smell that reached out to smite her and Barilan was almost a physical force. Talina retched uncontrollably and a fresh wave of anguish filled her, radiating out from the rent in her side.

It made no sound, but moved shockingly fast. It was all Talina could do to hold on as Barilan dodged a silent swing from the creature's tree-trunk arm.

If you would act, Talan, now is the time. Barilan's implacability carried clearly over the the their telepathic link and Talina remembered the staff. During her battle with Ciaran, her own staff had been literally chopped to pieces, and she inexplicably found herself holding the Staff of Elders. The Staff was grown from a living talonwood sapling, but had been frozen by a power she still didn't understand into a long, thin rod. She knew from experience that it would allow her to command the forest around them, at least in some measure, and the staff was definitely still alive, its essence linked to the Talonwood itself. She carried it now as if it were a part of her own body, and at Barilan's urging she raised it, attempting the same sort of attack that had served her so well against the Helinao only a few days before...